SOUL LOVE

A DAY IN THE LIFE – THE PREQUEL

SOUL LOVE SERIES

SIMON NORTHOUSE

FLABBERGASTED
PUBLISHING

For information about special discounts available for bulk purchases, sales promotions, fund-raising and educational needs contact admin@snorthouse.com or visit the Author's website at www.snorthouse.com or Facebook page https://www.facebook.com/simonnorthouse

Disclaimer: This is a work of fiction. Names, characters, businesses, places, events, locales, and incidents are either the products of the author's imagination or used in a fictitious manner. Any resemblance to actual persons, living or dead, or actual events is purely coincidental.

Published by Flabbergasted Publishing

First Edition

Kindle e-book ISBN-13:978-0-6485330-7-8

Paperback ISBN-13: 978-0-6485330-8-5

There is a sign up link at the end of this book to subscribe to my newsletter. I'll also gift you a couple of books.

TABLE OF CONTENTS

JIMMY'S DAY

I get a quick wash, dress then scoot down the stairs and into the kitchen. Sofe is sitting at the table reading a book whilst sipping on hot tea.

'Good morning, Sofe,' I say, full of the joys of Autumn.

'Is it?' she replies, sulkily.

'Yes, of course, it is. We're young, fighting fit and we're alive.' She ignores me. I look at the book title, "The Naked Ape." 'You're back onto the bodice rippers, then?' I laugh. She raises one eyebrow and peers at me above the book.

'It's about anthropology, actually.'

'Anthropology?'

'Yes, it's the study of...' I interrupt her as I flick the kettle on.

'I know what anthropology is. Just because you're a college pudding and I'm an unemployed dole scrounger doesn't mean that I'm thick you know. I have had an education.' She places her book on the table.

'Okay, what does it mean then?' I place a tea bag in a cup and await the kettle.

'It's the study of humans and our characteristics.' She smiles at me in a condescending manner.

'Very good. Although it is also the study of primates and hominids, of societies, language and behaviour.'

'That's what I said. What's for breakfast?' She returns to her reading.

'Ha! You'll be lucky. There's four slices of stale bread and one egg left.'

'Bugger, I'm ravenous. Time for a sleight of hand.' I pull a pint glass from the cupboard and fill it with tap water. I pour it down my throat as quickly as I can. Sofe stares at me with a puzzled expression.

'Does that really work?' she asks. I sit the glass in the sink and wipe some drops from my mouth.

'It certainly does. Tricks the body into thinking it's full, well, it lessens the hunger for a while. I wonder if I could patent it? It could be my pathway to millions.' She shakes her head.

'You can't patent an old wives tale.'

'Right, I'll have two slices of toast and you can have a fried egg sandwich,' I say, as I pour steaming hot water into my cup.

'Nah, you have the egg. I'll have toast.'

'No, you need the nutrition more than I do. You need to feed that brain of yours. All I'm doing today is signing on at the dole office. Do you want me to make it for you?' She makes a sudden jerking movement backwards and looks alarmed.

'No! The last time you made me a fried egg sandwich it was inedible.'

'Aw, come on, it wasn't that bad. It was maybe a little overdone, that's all.'

'Overdone? It was burnt. Thanks anyway, but I'll make my own.'

'Have we any jam left?'

'You may be able to scrape a bit from the bottom of the jar. Don't throw the tea bag away. We're nearly out. Just drop it into that tub on the side. We can reuse them.'

'Jesus, back to reusing old tea bags—things are tough this month,' I reply as I drop the bag into the plastic container that is already accumulating numerous soggy and sorry looking tea bags.

##

I sit at the table with my meagre rations and contemplate my day ahead.

'Hey, Sofe?'

'Yes, Jimmy?'

'You can't lend me two quid until my dole cheque arrives, can you?' She lets out a huff.

'Jimmy, I have four pounds left. There are two days to go until I get my money and you get your dole cheque. We have to eat. So, no, I can't lend you a couple of quid. Why? What do you want it for?'

'Bus fares and I'm meeting Marky in town at twelve for a pint.'

'Then definitely, no. I'm not subsidising your drinking habits while we have no food in the house.' I munch on my toast and wash it down with hot sugary tea.

'It's hardly a drinking habit. Beer has not passed my lips for the last ten days. Oh, well, I'll just have to walk. It keeps me fit.'

'Do you have to be so positive every day, especially in the mornings?'

'Why? Does it bother you?'

'Yes, it bloody well does! Does nothing ever get you down? You've no money, no job, we're living here in this nasty little house with nothing to eat and yet… you just seem to take it all in your stride. In fact, you seem to enjoy it.' I ponder for a moment.

'I don't really think about it. It is what it is. There's no point getting depressed about things, that won't change anything. There'll be better days ahead. Anyway, why wouldn't I be happy in the mornings? I get to look at your beautiful

3

face, your amazing body and discuss the meaning of life—what's not to like about that?'

'There's something wrong with you,' she scowls.

'As bad as things are, we always have...' She cuts me off.

'Each other, yes, I know. As you're forever reminding me.'

'No, I was going to say, as bad as things are, we always have tea.'

I set off on foot to the dole office. It's only a twenty-minute walk but then it's another good hour's stroll into Leeds City Centre to where I'm meeting Marky.

There's a cold chill in the air but the smell of Autumn more than makes up for the minor discomfort. There's something real and earthy about this time of year. When I was a kid, it was my second favourite part of the calendar, behind Christmas. Chumping for firewood, building a Guy Fawkes and saving pocket money for Bangers, Little Demons and Screechers. Before Bonfire Night we would have Mischievous Night which grew bigger and wilder each year. When I was young the pinnacle of our exploits would be to knock on people's doors and run away. We'd watch and giggle at the homeowner's expressions as they came to the threshold. From there we moved on to putting dog crap into a brown paper bag. We'd sneak up the garden path and place our surprise on the front doorstep. One of us would set it alight as the other rapped angrily on the door. Then off we'd skedaddle to watch proceedings. The laughter was the best kind of laughter. The type where you are desperately trying not to laugh lest you give your hidden position away. There was no funnier sight than witnessing a middle-aged dour Yorkshire man jump up and down on that paper bag whilst cursing his unknown tormentors. Then the best part. With exclamations of "Blood and thunder" or "Buggering little tits!", the man's wife would arrive at the door and admonish her husband for having dog shit on his shoe.

When we got into our teen's things turned even more unruly. We'd walk on top of car roofs, throw bangers at each other and aim Screechers at people's bedroom windows. One year we were chased all over town by the police. There

4

was about ten of us in the gang, half of whom they arrested. Me, Marky and a few of the other lads avoided capture but it was a close call. No one was charged, but the police visited the parents to issue a lecture knowing full well the parents would administer their own kangaroo court and swift justice. Ah, happy days! I'll be turning nineteen in December and I'm a lot more mature now, so no more mischievous nights for me or Marky.

There's a massive queue at the dole office. The line snakes out of the building and down the high street. There's good natured banter between most of the men and a few women. I strike up a conversation with an old guy who looks about sixty but is probably in his late forties. It does it to you, living here, getting old before your time. Mind you, he's a chain-smoker and has trembling hands, so I assume he's a big drinker as well.

'Heard of any jobs going?' I ask him. He holds his smoke between two fingers and his thumb then takes an almighty drag on it.

'I heard about a job the other day, at Cotterills, packing cashews that get shipped out to Saudi Arabia.'

'Oh, yeah,' I reply. 'Did you get an interview?'

'Sure did. Not only that, but they offered me the job!'

'Really?' I respond, unsure why he's standing here in the dole queue if they'd offered him the job. 'Why didn't you take it?'

'They were paying peanuts!' he bursts out laughing and coughing at the same time. I walked right into that one. That's the thing with these guys, they are as sharp as tacks. They have nothing. They have no future. But, they always have a laugh.

Eventually, I move inside the building but there are still over eighty people in front of me. They have five kiosks open to deal with everyone but the queue moves painfully slow. Now and then, an argument will erupt as one of the dole officers tells someone the bad news. Maybe they will receive a reduced payment for failing to comply with some arbitrary rule. Or maybe someone has grassed them up for doing work that was not declared. Voices are raised, expletives are fired like a machine gun and the recalcitrant miscreant is sent on his way with a bundle of forms to take home and fill in.

I've been coming here every fortnight since I left school. Two and a half years of queuing, form filling, of being hauled into the supervisor's office to explain what action I'm taking to find work. I learnt early on to bite my tongue. If you come the smartarse or give them a hard time, then there's always payback. The dole cheque that doesn't arrive as it should on Thursday morning. Then back to the dole office you trudge to find out why.

"Oh, it must have been delayed in the post. If it hasn't arrived by tomorrow come back and see us." When it still hasn't arrived it's back again, to be handed another excuse. This now means I have to spend the weekend without two beans to rub together. When it still hasn't materialised by Monday you return for another visit. They finally figure out what the problem is. They tell me I'm no longer unemployed which comes as a bit of a shock to me as I'm sure I am. I spend the next thirty minutes explaining they've made a mistake, I have no job, I am still unemployed. Another hour passes before they realise their mistake and admit that they got me mixed up with someone else. My name is Jimmy Hooper, and they had got it confused with J Cooper—or so they say. Yes, I soon realised it's all a big game. You need to act like those herd of sheep they have on the TV. The ones that are rounded up by the sheepdog as the farmer lets out shrill whistles and shouts things like, "come around, boy, come around." The sheep know the drill and they almost walk themselves into the pen. Well, it's the same at this place. Keep your head down. Act polite but don't be a sycophant. Give them the answers they want to hear. Offer no more information than the bare essentials. Sign your name and get the hell out of there and pray that your dole cheque drops through the letterbox in two days time.

The chain-smoker is up next and I say goodbye to him as he disappears into the little cubicle. No sooner is he out of sight than I hear the woman behind the counter question him.

'Mr Braithwaite, it has come to our attention that you have received payment for work in the last fortnight,' she begins in a loud whisper.

'Nay, lass. That's not right. Who told you that?' he replies with a worried voice.

'I'm sorry, but I cannot divulge that information. We believe that you have been doing window cleaning on the Ganner Estate. As you are well aware...'

'Ah, no, you don't understand. I have an old aunty who lives on the Ganners and every few weeks I pop around there and clean her windows. She doesn't pay me though. She's family. All I get out of it is a cup of tea and a digestive biscuit.'

'Mr Braithwaite, you must have a lot of old aunties that live on the Ganners. Last week alone you cleaned the windows of over twenty houses.'

'Who's feeding you this rubbish!' he says, raising his voice.

'I'm not at liberty to divulge that information. We are suspending your benefits pending further investigation.'

'No! You can't do that! I have a disabled wife. We have no food in the house! I have bills to pay, otherwise they'll cut me off!'

'I'm sorry, Mr Braithwaite, but as I said...' And so it goes on. I feel sorry for the old bastard. He'll have no money for his smokes or drink. I know what you're thinking—if he's signing on then he shouldn't be spending his money on cigarettes and alcohol, right? Well, yes... and no. From an early age, they bombard us with cigarette and alcohol advertising. Get them while they're young. Every major sporting event is sponsored by a tobacco giant or a thirsty brewery. Billboards, newspapers, TV adverts and TV shows all tell us that it's "cool" to smoke, that real men drink. Most people get sucked in, after all, if advertising didn't work, they wouldn't use it. That's okay, while you're working, you can afford it. But when you're thrown onto the scrap heap, you're suddenly expected to kick your habits. It's hard to do, especially when it's probably the only comfort you get.

I'm up next. The middle aged woman behind the glass, stares at me. I've encountered her many times over the years and she is one cold ice cube. She shows no emotion, she's like a robot. She can read people as well, and has a mean bullshit detector.

'Name.'

'Jimmy Hooper.'

'Mr Hooper, have you been available for work in the last fortnight?'

'Yes.'

'Have you been employed in any capacity and, or received payment by way of money or in-kind for that work?' You see what I mean? She's a crafty one. That's a loaded question. It's two questions in one, designed to confuse, but I'm up to speed with her little word games.

'No, I have not been employed in any capacity. No, I have received no payment by way of money or in-kind.' She looks down her nose at me disbelievingly, even though it's the Gospel truth. She waits, trying to unnerve me. I stare back at her blankly, poker-faced. She pushes a form across the counter.

'Sign here,' she commands, expressionless. I scribble my signature and push the form back to her. 'Next!' she yells as I breathe a sigh of relief and hurriedly exit the building.

I'm making my way through Chapeltown, on foot. It's got a bad reputation because of the riots in 1981. It has a large Caribbean population and one of the highest unemployment rates in the city. Mix that with racial tension, poverty and the heavy-handedness of the police and it is a tinderbox awaiting the next spark. I like it though. There's always something going on, it has an edge, an atmosphere. Real people live here, real people with real lives. This isn't sweet, boring suburbia. As I walk towards a row of shops, I hear reggae music blasting out from a high window of a terraced house across the road. I spot a familiar face emerge from a grocery store laden with bulging plastic bags. I pull my camera from around my neck and get a few shots of him before he spots me.

'Hey, Jimmy, put that camera away,' he shouts at me in his Caribbean accent, grinning as he does so. I walk up to him as he places a couple of bags on the ground. We do the old hand slap back and forth.

'Nelson, I'm glad to see you're a new age man. Doing the shopping, nice touch.' He grins and laughs.

'I always do the shopping in my house and also all the cooking. I'm in the wrong profession. I should have been a chef.' Nelson works the bar at one of the best nightclubs in the city.

'It's never too late, Nelson. Maybe you should open up your own restaurant or café?' I suggest as Nelson picks up his carrier bags. He looks at me thoughtfully.

'Hmm, you know what, Jimmy, that is not a bad idea. Although, the climate is not right for opening up a business at the moment. Most businesses are closing down. Look at this high street. The record shop has gone. The little café on the corner closed its doors last week and there's even a rumour the Laundromat is about to close down. Times are tough Jimmy, times are tough. So, how come I haven't seen you in the Granary for a while?'

'Lack of funds,' I reply.

'Oh, come on, Jimmy, you always sweet talk your way in for nothing and you know I'll always give you your first drink for free.' I smile and pat him on the back of the shoulder.

'Yeah, I know, Nelson. There haven't been any bands playing that tickle my fancy, lately. It's all that electronic synth shit. But, don't you worry, I'll be back.' He looks surprised.

'So, you haven't heard the news?'

'What news?'

'Your mates, The Hipnotikz are playing the Granary this evening? The band that was due to play cancelled. Iris rang Macca and asked if The Hipnotikz could stand in at short notice.'

'Oh, really? Well, in that case, I may pop down there tonight.' I know I won't go. I don't fancy another good hours walk home after midnight.

We chew the cud for another five minutes then say our farewells. I like Nelson; he's honest, hardworking and his smile is infectious. I make a mental note to check out the upcoming gigs at the Granary for the forthcoming month. I look at my watch and realise that if I don't get a move on I'm going to be late meeting Marky. It's time to jog, which seems to be my main mode of transport these days. Ah, well, it won't always be like this—I guess.

##

We emerge from the pub, or wine bar as it is called now, and I walk with Marky for a while until he turns left down the Headrow, toward the law courts and I turn right and head towards New Briggate.

'I'll see you in the Granary, tonight!' I yell out to him. He raises his hand and disappears into the crowd. As I pass the John Lewis department store, I notice a promotion that is being advertised. It's a cheese company that has a new product line and they're offering a free tasting. These are the opportunities you've got to look out for. I go inside and make my way to the food department. It's busy but I spot two tables set up with women dressed in white coats sporting white hats. I saunter over to them. One is an older woman, someone's granny no doubt, and the other is a young girl, a very attractive young girl, probably about my age. Time for the Jimmy charm. I walk up to her and offer up my sweetest smile. She reciprocates.

'May I taste your cheese, young lady?'

'Yes, you may.' She turns around and picks up a paper plate containing four small cubes of cheese with toothpicks stuck through them. Would you like a cracker with that?' she asks.

'No, I'll take them straight.' I place the first cube into my mouth and chew, slowly savouring the taste. I pull a thoughtful expression. 'Hmm, creamy yet with a hint of elderflower and a soupcon of blackberry.' The cheese girl giggles.

'A soup what?' she asks

'Soupcon, a small amount.'

'Oh,' she smiles as I place an orange coloured cube into my mouth. I chew again.

'Ah! Now this has a more robust flavour. I can imagine hairy farmhands and milk maids with huge jugs—of milk—striding across lush green fields.' The cheese girl flutters her eyelashes at me. I finish the cheese off and make more inane quips to a captive audience. I hand her the plate. 'Do you think I could try another plate, this time with crackers?' I enquire. She glances furtively across to the older woman who is busy with a gentleman who for some bizarre reason, is wearing a bowler hat.

'Well, we're only supposed to hand out one plate per customer...' I push my bottom lip out and pull a sad expression. 'But, I'll make an exception,' she continues. I finish off the plate of cheese and crackers.

'What's your name?' I ask.

'Sheryl,' she replies.

'Ah, Sheryl, one of my favourite names,' I grin.

'Oh, you're full of shit, aren't you,' she laughs.

'Yes, I am. How about you and me go out, some time?' I suggest. She looks sad.

'Sorry, but I have a boyfriend.'

'I'm not asking you to marry me... not yet, anyway. Okay, how about I give you my telephone number and when or if you split up with your lucky boyfriend, call me?' She pulls a pen from her jacket pocket in a shot and hands me the cheese maker's business card. I scribble my number on the back and hand it to her.

'Jimmy,' she says.

'Yep, that's me. Nice to meet you Sheryl.' I'm about to turn to leave when I spot a small refrigerator at the side of the table.

'What's in the fridge?'

'What do you think? Cheese of course.'

'Hey, I've just had an idea. My uncle owns four successful delicatessens around the city. How about you give me a few blocks of cheese and he can give samples out at his shops?' She looks a little nervous.

'Erm, I'm not sure...'

'I'm telling you, he sells a ton of cheese. If you could get your product into his shops, you'd be onto a winner. I'll also make sure he mentions your name when he places an order.' She noticeably brightens. I feel like such a heel for lying to her.

'Okay, I'll just check with Maude.' She wanders over to her older partner and both women engage in a serious discussion. Sheryl keeps nodding my way. She makes her way back to me sporting a huge grin.

'Okay, Maude says you can have four blocks of each type. I'll put them in a carrier bag for you.' Sixteen blocks of cheese! I've scored big time. As I leave, I call out to her,

'Remember, when you've had enough of lover boy, give me a call. I'll be waiting for you.' She waves at me and shouts,

'See you, Jimmy!' I set off on the long walk home and suddenly realise that sixteen blocks of cheese weighs quite a lot and my arms are already tiring. I walk past the Odeon Cinema, cross the busy road then notice a large throng of schoolchildren waiting at the bus stop where I'd normally catch my bus—if I had any money to spare. I can't bear the thought of breaking into the money that Marky gave me in the pub. A teacher is trying unsuccessfully to corral the kids into some sort of order.

'Come on, children! Orderly line, single file! The bus is here. Keep away from the road. Stevens, you damn fool! You haven't got the brains you were born with! Now, move back and stop pushing!' he yells at one boy in an exasperated manner. I watch as the bus pulls up. Despite the teachers protestations the group of kids swarm forward knocking him out of the way as they invade the bus like a horde of mice. I see my opportunity and tag along behind them, half-crouching as I ascend onto the bus platform. The kids are laughing and screaming, the teacher is yelling and the bus driver is completely overwhelmed. I slip past him as he chunters with the teacher. I skip upstairs and sit at the very front of the bus on the left-hand side. It's the only spot on the bus that is out of the line of sight of the driver's security mirrors. It's also the best place for spotting any Ticket Inspectors awaiting at future stops. Those guys are few and far between but they are ruthless at handing out on-the-spot fines.

The bus trundles on for a good twenty minutes and I begin to feel very drowsy. There's something comforting about travelling along on a double-decker. The familiar rattle and hum of the chairs, the distant drone of the diesel engine, the ding-ding of the bell.

I wake with a start as the bus blares its horn at someone or something. I stare out of the window and yawn. The bus slows and manoeuvres towards the pavement. Standing at the bus stop is a tall man wearing a long green overcoat and a peaked cap.

'Shit! Ticket Inspector. Fuck it!' I look under my seat and spot a few discarded ticket stubs. I pick two up and stuff them into my back pocket. I hear the swish of the bus doors, immediately followed by a gruff, authoritarian voice.

'Ticket Inspector! Have your tickets at the ready please.' I'm only two stops from home. I stand up and gaze down the stairwell for a moment. I glance over my shoulder at the bus's progress. One more set of traffic lights, a roundabout, then it's the next stop. I wait. Through the lights, we go. As the bus slows down to circumnavigate the roundabout, I see the Ticket Inspector climb the stairs. I press the red button twice and the bell rings out. I begin my descent and meet the Ticket Inspector half-way down the stairs.

'Tickets, please,' he commands. I smile at him and pull the two ticket stubs from my pocket and hand them over.

'Hey, pal,' I whisper as I nod my head to the side, 'there's a guy sitting at the back of the bus who's slashing the seats with a penknife.' The Ticket Inspector, who is busily squinting at my tickets, stops and suddenly looks concerned at this false information.

'Wait here,' he barks at me. As he bustles past, I feel the bus lean sharply to the left. I bounce down the stairs and ring the bell again as the bus pulls up at its stop. There's the swoosh of pneumatics as the double doors fling open.

'Hey! Get back here!' yells the disembodied voice of the Inspector. I hear his feet come thumping down the steps. As I'm about to leap from the platform, I feel a hand on my shoulder. I half turn and punch it away, then jump to the pavement and sprint. The Inspector follows me but it's no contest, even though I'm carrying a half-gross of cheese under one arm.

'I know your face!' he yells at me. I'm in fits of laughter as I dart up a side road and away from the bus route.

MARKY'S DAY

I'm in Flip Of The Coin wine bar, also known as Tossers, waiting for my best pal, Jimmy. He's already ten minutes late which is most out of character for him and I feel a twang of anxiety. I head back to the bar with my empty pint glass and place it on the counter.

'Same again?' asks Jenny, the landlady of this fine establishment.

'Yes, please, Jenny. And take one for Jimmy. No doubt he'll be skint as usual.'

'More than likely. I feel sorry for him sometimes. He's a bright lad, I can't understand why he can't get a job,' she comments as she places my refill on the bar. I hand her a fiver and she turns towards the till.

'Because, Jenny, there's three and a half million Jimmies looking for work and no jobs. Government policy; create mass unemployment, drive wages down and smash the unions.' She hands me my change.

'Yeah, yeah. Play another record, Marky. It's a worldwide recession, you can't blame it all at the feet of the Tories.'

'Can't I?' I snap back. The indifference and apathy of the British people never fails to astound me. As long as they have their smokes, beer, tabloid gutter press and crappy soap operas, they'll put up with anything. Millions on the dole queue, thousands becoming homeless every day, interest rates at 9% with mortgage rates at 18%, we know who's making a killing there, and an emerging police state and what do the Brits do? Nothing! If there was a sudden beer shortage or a main character from a soap opera was killed off, they'd be marching on the Houses Of Parliament demanding immediate action. Well, I for one won't be letting this great nation slide into the Conservative abyss without a fight. There are murmurings and mutterings. *Some* people are beginning to organise, to question the status quo. I've noticed it just recently, blowing gently through the air carried on thermals of discontent and desperation. What we need is a mass strike. If the miners, the dockers, the steelworkers and the railways came out together, then this country would grind to a halt. I reckon the government would last maybe a fortnight, tops. They'd have to back down, change tack. They'd be irrevocably weakened. If the Labour Party could grow some Marxist balls and sell their message in a coherent fashion then this shower of shit that runs the country could be gone by December. Now that would be a Christmas present to savour.

'Oh, give me two bags of smoky bacon, as well.' Jenny places the crisps on the counter, picks some coins from my change and moves on to the next customer. It's beginning to fill up with the suits from the financial district. How come they aren't feeling the so-called recession the same as everyone else? They all still appear to be cashed up with their calfskin wallets, Armani suits and Gucci shoes—fucking parasites. When the great revolt eventuates, these bastards need to be set to work on a chain gang. Give them five years of hard manual labour. Let them dig the roads, empty the bins, nurse the sick, dig the fucking coal—see what real life is like.

I sit back down at the table and light a cigarette as I check my watch again. He's now fifteen minutes late.

I met Jimmy on my first day at Junior school. It was playtime when I spotted this kid bouncing a tennis ball against a large stone wall. He was catching it one-handed. First in the left, next bounce in the right hand. I watched for a while until I got bored. I timed my run perfectly and darted in front of him just as the ball was heading his way. I caught it and began to run. I was laughing like a drain as he chased me. My God, he was fast. He tackled me to the ground and tried to wrestle the ball from me. Unfortunately, I was born with a bit of a short fuse and the red mist descended. I began to beat the shit out of him. He didn't offer much

16

resistance, just sort of curled up in a ball looking terrified. Then he began to cry. I recall the feelings that flooded through me. I felt like a right bastard. There he was, as happy as a lark, minding his own business, probably a little scared and anxious on his first day at school.

I stopped hitting him, bent down, stroked his head and said sorry. I offered him my hand then pulled him to his feet. I pulled a crisp, neatly ironed handkerchief from my shorts and handed it to him. He wiped his tears away, blew his nose on it and passed it back. I patted him on the shoulder and he smiled. I told him that if he was ever being bullied by anyone, then he had to come to me and I'd sort it for him. That was that. We've been best mates ever since, well more like brothers. There's nothing I wouldn't do for Jimmy—nothing. Ah, here he comes now, trotting down the steps with a big beam on his face. Just seeing his smile lightens my load. I point towards the bar.

'There's one waiting for you,' I shout. He gives me the thumbs up. I watch as Amy, Jenny's daughter, serves him. He's giving her his chat-up lines. He's a bit of a ladies' man is young Jimmy. They all seem to fall for him and why wouldn't they. He's good looking, super fit, has a beautiful personality, and he's always wearing that damn smile! The problem with Jimmy though, is that he's soft. Oh, I don't mean at fighting, he can mostly hold his own in that department, although he's no Muhammad Ali. No, what I mean is that he only sees the good in people. He loves everyone and doesn't mind telling them. Sometimes it's like sharing a pint with JC! He throws Amy one more of his boyish grins whilst flashing his pearly whites then makes his way over to me. He doesn't see it, but Amy is standing gawping at him as he turns his back to her. She'll start fucking drooling in a minute.

'Hey, Jimmy, where've you been, man? I was getting worried about you.' He places his pint on the table as I hold out my fist which he bumps with his.

'Yeah, sorry, Marky. Had to jog into town, I'm skint. Plus the dole queue took forever this morning. It gets longer every fortnight,' he explains as he sips gently on his lager.

'Too fucking right it does! And we all know why!' He shakes his head at me.

'Not now, Marky. It's a beautiful Autumn's day. I get my dole cheque the day after tomorrow and I think I might have a chance with Amy. I'm not in the mood for a political lecture—just let me enjoy the moment.' See what I mean? Disaffected, indifferent, unmotivated—the Great British sleep-a-thon. I relent.

'I think you've got more than a chance,' I reply. He puts his pint down, tears open a packet of crisps and crams a handful into his mouth.

'Nah, I need to turn up the charm offensive,' he offers in reply.

'Mate, you could come in here and say nothing and she'd still have the hots for you. Just ask her out and be done with it?' He chews away thoughtfully for a moment.

'Where would I take her? I have no money.'

'Fucking hell, Jim! You can be thick sometimes. You've got your own pad, take her there. Her bloody mother owns this pub—hang out here. Go for a walk. Take her to the gallery. Trail around the shops, window shopping. Use your imagination.' He takes his camera from around his neck and shoots a quick glance over his shoulder. Right on cue, Amy sends him a telegraphed smile, flutters her eyelashes and swishes her hair back.

'Hmm,' he says, 'I'm not sure she's that interested.' Sometimes I could slap him. 'So, what have you been working on?' he asks.

'Bloody court duty again, I'm sick of it. Dave Dee says it's a good training ground for me. I can learn how to detect when someone's lying or covering something up. He says it will sharpen my reporter's intuition. It shortens my bloody life, I can tell you that much.' He laughs and takes another swig of his drink.

'It can't all be boring, there must be some interesting bits, you know, grisly murders and all that?' I stub my cigarette out in the ashtray.

'Nah, he won't let me do murder cases, yet. Not until I'm qualified. All I get is the crap. Dole cheats, bad debtors, the odd flasher here and there and the occasional armed robbery.'

18

We chat on for another fifteen minutes. I buy us both another pint and notice that I'm due back in court in ten minutes.

'Oh, Jim, I got a call from Macca this morning. The Hipnotikz are playing the Granary tonight—you up for it?'

'Yeah, I know. I bumped into Nelson on the way. No, I can't afford it,' he replies glumly.

'Aw, come on,' I encourage as I dig into my pockets and pull a roll of notes out. 'Here, take this fiver.' Jimmy shakes his head.

'No, Marky. You're forever giving me money or buying me pints, it's not right.'

'If the positions were reversed would you do the same for me?'

'Of course, I would, you know that.'

'Well then, what's the problem?'

'I can't justify it. Sofe has four quid left for food for the next two days. I can't go for a night out and blow a fiver when we're both starving.' I pull out another fiver and throw it on the table. 'No! Definitely not, Marky—no way.'

'That's an advance on your dole money. You can pay me back Thursday. Five for food and five for a good time.'

'It's not just that. It means walking all the way back home, then walking back into town, then back home after midnight.' I stand up and finish the dregs of my pint.

'Don't talk wet. I'll call Macca, you can roadie for them. He'll pick you up and drop you off. That means you'll get into the gig for free, no doubt they'll shout you a few pints and you're chauffeured around. Hey, you could ask Amy if she wants to come along.' He throws another glance over his shoulder.

'Nah, gigs are never good for dating. You can't hear yourself speak. Plus, I think I might need to win her over a bit more first.' I roll my eyes.

'Jesus, you're a lost cause. Right, come on, take the money. We'll have a good night out, maybe a curry for supper—whaddya say?' He finally smiles and says,

'Fuck it! Why not.' I pick up the two fivers and stick them in his jacket. He grabs his camera, removes the lens cap and takes a photo of me pulling a silly face. I hold out my fist to him.

'Okay, comrade, I'll see you tonight in the Granary.' He bumps my fist.

'No, hang on, I'm leaving as well. I'll walk with you,' he replies as he hurriedly downs his pint. As we walk out of the bar, he calls out to Amy.

'See you later, Amy!' She shoots him a giant beam which flies completely over his head.

'See you soon, Jimmy!' she calls out expectantly. Poor girl, I can see she will have to make the first move.

It was a bad idea knocking back three pints at lunchtime. I spend the rest of the afternoon trying to stop myself from nodding off. Surprising, really, as it's a fascinating case involving an accountant who embezzled his client's money. I've had more fun cutting my toenails. Eventually, the crusty old magistrate adjourns proceedings for the day. He looks about as enthused as me.

I dawdle along the city streets looking in shop windows trying to kill some time. I think about Jimmy and his predicament. There must be something I can do to help him. You need a little luck in this world and it appears someone else got Jimmy's share. I was lucky, or rather I made my own luck. When I was still at school, I got a two-week work experience placement at the Yorkshire Evening Standard. I knew the very first morning I walked into the newsroom, this was the world for me. The buzz, the excitement, old craggy faces smoking Woodbines and slurping on strong black coffee. It had an atmosphere that filled me with energy— it still does. News is not about yesterday or tomorrow—it's about the "right now". It's living in the moment—apart from the law courts which is not like living at all.

For those two weeks, I didn't stop. I did photocopying, ran errands, made people tea and coffee, collected their lunch orders from the takeaway shops and bakeries. I made sure I struck up a relationship with everyone. I even washed old Bulldog's car for him. Call it arse-licking or whatever you want but it worked. When I left school I pestered Dave Dee for a job. He said, no. He said I needed a degree. I offered to work for him for free, to gain more experience. Again, he said no. Eventually, they stopped me from entering the building. So, I'd wait outside and collar Dave as he left work—and Dave works long hours, let me tell you. After a couple of weeks of this incessant barrage, he finally cracked. Who could resist the Marky charm?

For a full month I threw myself into anything and everything they asked me to do. I even did things I wasn't asked to do, such as cleaning the toilets, emptying ashtrays and sweeping the floor. Then, one day, Dave was making his way out of the door. He was on his way to interview a woman about her teenage son who had gone missing. He asked me if I'd like to come along. I jumped at the chance. I still remember his words to me as we got out of the car and knocked on the woman's front door.

"Marky, keep fucking quiet. Look, listen and learn." He was a master. He got so much out of the woman by gentle questioning and a good dose of empathy. It was traumatic to witness another person's fear, loss, their impending sense of doom. Dave ran the piece on the front page of the next day's edition—after a battle with Bulldog, who didn't think it warranted the position. The woman's son was found two days later, floating in the River Aire. The coroner recorded an open verdict. Dave went back to see the mother to offer his condolences. He also attended the funeral service. Yep, Dave is a hard bastard, he doesn't suffer fools gladly, but he has a heart.

Not long after, I arrived in the morning, early as usual and there was a hell of a row going off in Bulldog's office. It was Dave and Bulldog having a real old ding dong. I assumed it was about some story or such. Eventually, Dave emerged, red in the face. He looked at me and said,

"Marky, Bulldog wants to see you." I assumed they were getting rid of their free help. Bulldog offered me a job as a Cadet Reporter. That's what they were arguing about. Dave was fighting my corner. That's the type of guy he is.

21

##

I'm back in the newsroom and have just finished typing my copy of the day's proceedings. If anyone suffers from insomnia, then all they need to do is read my little piece. They'll be pushing out the "zzz" in seconds. I walk over to Dave Dee and slip it into his in-tray.

'Have you got anything else for me?' I ask. He's got his head down and his red pen is going nineteen to the dozen. In his left hand is a smouldering cigarette, mostly ash.

'No,' he says without looking up. I glance at the clock. There are still two hours to go before knocking off time. It's quiet in the newsroom and I reckon this is as good a time as any.

'Hey, Dave?' There's no reply. 'Dave?' I wait a few moments. 'Dave?' He lets out a huff and throws his pen down.

'Fucking hell, Marky, what now?' he shouts. I smile at him and he relaxes back into his chair. 'Here we go, I know that look of yours, Marky. It means you're after something. If it's about the law courts, then you're wasting your time. You're there all week. Get it?'

'No, it's not about the law courts. Do you remember me telling you about my best mate, Jimmy?' He looks puzzled.

'Vaguely. What about him?'

'Well, he's a bloody great photographer…' I don't get any further.

'No! Definitely not! We've got one staffer and enough freelancers to sink a boat. We don't need any more.' He looks at the clock. 'Right, go fuck off home and give me some peace. I'll see you tomorrow.'

As I make my way out of the building, I don't feel defeated. It's the first skirmish. I've planted the seed, it just needs a little watering and TLC. I've got time and Jimmy's got time. It will be a war of attrition, my favourite type of war and there'll only be one winner.

22

SOFE'S DAY

'No, I was going to say, as bad as things are, we always have tea.'

'Haha, you're hilarious,' I reply with my best deadpan look, trying not to smile. He abruptly pushes his chair back, stands and exits the kitchen into the hallway. I see him pick up his camera, throw it around his neck and put on his blue Harrington jacket. He marches back into the kitchen, slaps his hands around my cheeks and gives me a big smacker on the forehead.

'Right, I'll be off, Sofe. Love you, but got to leave you. I'll be back.' I slap his arms away, as I always do and scowl at him—I'm a good actress.

'Good riddance,' I reply, in a truculent, annoyed fashion. As he nears the front door he turns and laughs.

'Come on, Sofe, you know you don't mean that,' he states with an impish grin. Then he's gone.

No, I don't mean it. The walls visibly shift three feet inwards as he departs—my prison—my tomb. When he's here I feel safe, warm, invigorated—alive. When he leaves a heavy dark cloud descends. We've been flatmates for over eighteen months and there's nothing between us—I mean sexually. It is a marriage of convenience. We are like brother and sister and that's how it will stay until I've passed my degree in another nine months.

There are nights I've been tempted. As I toss and turn in my cold, soulless room, I contemplate creeping up the stairs to his, opening the door and slipping into bed with him. I work him hard with my hand as he sleeps, then I straddle him. Oh, my, how I dream of this. It will happen—eventually. But, first and foremost, I must concentrate on my studies. Nothing, not even Jimmy, will push me off course.

When I have my degree, I will make my move—but not until then. Yes, I know he has girlfriends; he tells me all the details, oblivious to my ultimate intent. But, the girlfriends, they come and go, nothing serious. It does not bother me. I hope that he is gaining experience in becoming a better and considerate lover. I do have one fear though. What if he should meet "her", the "one", and fall in love—true love, not lust nor infatuation? What would I do then? Jimmy is mine, always has been since the very first day we moved into this vermin-infested, decrepit house.

No, he does not know it yet—but please, God, just give me nine more months then me and Jimmy will be together in the fullest sense—and forever. He needs someone like me to look out for him and I need his unrelenting positivity to buoy my dark days. We were made for each other—his Yin against my Yang, my logic against his intuition. It is the perfect marriage.

##

I work on my latest thesis, "Dysfunctional Behaviour In The Pubescent Mind", sounds riveting, right? Well, if you are studying psychology, believe me, it is. My stomach aches for food and I feel light-headed. I go to the kitchen and try Jimmy's trick. I gulp down a full pint of tepid tap water as fast as possible, then make myself a cup of weak tea with the second-hand tea bags. The bugger is right, it works. Not only does my hunger subside but by re-hydrating, my thinking becomes clearer. I make good progress with my thesis and just about finish it when I hear the front door open, then close, followed by the sound of Jimmy's laughter. I open my bedroom door and stare at him. He's bent over panting and giggling, a plastic carrier bag dangles from his hand.

'What's happened now?' I ask.

24

'Oh, I just did a runner from a Ticket Inspector.' He stands upright and smiles at me as he makes his way into the kitchen. He drops the bag on the table.

'What's in there?' I enquire.

'Cheese, Sofe. A lot of fucking cheese.'

'You didn't steal it, did you?' He looks at me aghast.

'Sofe, how could you! I'm not a thief, I've never stolen anything in my life,' he exclaims with mock hurt.

'What about the records from that second-hand shop in the Merrion Centre?' He grabs a glass of water and slugs it down.

'That's not stealing. I'm just giving them a good holiday for a while. At some point, I'll return them.' I cross my arms and lean against the wall.

'And what about the loaves of bread, the bottle of whisky, the fillet steak that you've nabbed from the supermarket over the years? Plus all the rest. Are you going to hand them back as well?' He puts the glass down and stares at me as though deep in thought.

'I'm actually saving the taxpayer a ton of money,' he eventually replies with a smile.

'How so?'

'Well, if they rushed me into hospital with malnutrition, imagine how much it would cost to keep me in there—thousands or at least hundreds a day.'

'You don't need whisky to live,' I persist.

'Try telling that to the Scots. Anyway, that was a present for Marky's birthday.'

'Did you tell him you'd nicked it from Safeways?'

'I did. He said it tasted even better knowing that. Supermarkets are capitalist pimps, according to Marky. Anyway, I got the cheese from a rather attractive young lady in John Lewis. They were launching a new cheese. I told her my uncle owned a string of famous delicatessens, and I'd pass them on to him to hand out.'

'So, you lied?'

'No, I had a creative moment.'

'I think I will write my next thesis about you. I'll call it, "Delusion, Denial and Overconfidence in Teenagers." I reckon I'd get a high distinction for it.' He walks back to the table and empties the cheese blocks out onto the surface. 'Christ, that will last us a year!' I cry. He rubs his chin and ponders a while.

'Can you freeze cheese?'

'Yes,' I say as I open the freezer door and begin stacking the blocks inside.

'Hey, Sofe, not only that, but look at this,' he shouts, excitedly. I turn as he pulls two five pound notes from his pocket and slaps them down on the table. 'We, my beautiful little flatmate, are going to the supermarket right now! With your four quid and my five quid that gives us nine pounds!'

'Good at maths, were you?' He ignores me.

'The other fiver is for a night out for both of us.' He grins like he's just won the football pools.

'Where did you get it from?'

'Marky bunged me five for tonight and lent me another five until my dole cheque arrives. The Hipnotikz are playing the Granary this evening, you up for it?'

'Five pounds won't go far between the two of us.' He laughs as I shut the freezer door.

'Ha, that's where you're wrong. We are roadies so we get in for free and I'm sure the lads will buy us a few beers for our help. If we're lucky, we may even have a bit left over for an onion bhaji each after the gig.'

'And how do we get home? I'm not bloody walking at that time of night.' He comes over to me and grabs my left cheek between his thumb and forefinger and wiggles it, as you would a cherubic baby.

26

'You shall be transported in a crystal carriage to the ball—well, Macca's transit van to the gig. Come on, what do you say?' I hit his hand away from my cheek.

'Hmm, maybe. I have just finished my latest thesis so the pressure's off for the moment.'

'Come on, Sofe! Let your hair down for once. All work and no play makes Jill a dull boy.'

'Girl. Okay, yeah, I could do with a break.' He grabs me by the back of the head and plants a big smacker on my forehead. 'Stop it! You weirdo!'

##

I slap him on the arm. 'Put that back,' I admonish. He reluctantly replaces the most expensive brand of chocolate biscuits back on the shelf. I pick up a home brand packet of Arrowroot biscuits. 'These are one-fifth the price,' I explain, as I drop them into my basket.

'Yeah, and for a very good reason—they taste like shit,' he complains. He's hopeless at shopping on a budget. When we first moved in together, I once made the foolish mistake of letting him do the shopping solo. He blew twenty pounds on chocolate bars, beer, fillet steak and some Stilton cheese. Since then I either do the shopping alone or I chaperone him—he cannot be trusted.

'The problem with you, Jimmy, is that you shop like a millionaire.'

'I am a millionaire—I've just got a cash flow problem at the minute,' he grins. 'Hey, Sofe, what about some meat?'

'Hmm, maybe. We'll check the prices out.'

'I fancy beef.'

'No, too expensive. Chicken will do.'

'Breast?'

'No, thigh. It's cheaper and more tender.'

'But I'm a breast man.'

'Don't be smutty.'

As we make our way through the fruit and vegetable section I notice a cabbage going for half-price. 'Oh, that's a bargain. Just fifteen pence, we'll take that.'

'It's all yellow,' he moans. I peel a few leaves back and show him the verdant green below. 'Hmm, okay. I'll look forward to a gourmet meal of cabbage one night.' I laugh at him.

'Ever had cabbage leaves stuffed with aromatic rice with a thick tomato sauce over the top?' He shakes his head. 'Well, you're in for a treat.'

As we walk around I sort of act annoyed with him but I enjoy it, really. People sometimes look at us, as though we are a couple, and it gives me little butterflies inside. We pick up some rice, split peas, pearl barley, lentils and two bags of flour on special.

'Are you keeping count?' I ask him as he tries adding the prices up on a little notepad.

'Erm, yeah, that comes to eight pounds fifty-two… I think,' he replies as he scratches the side of his cheek with the butt of the pencil.

'No, I make it eight pounds forty. We have sixty pence left. That will get us three packets of dried macaroni and we've already got the cheese.'

'Erm, no, I've definitely added this up correctly. We'll get to the checkout then have to return something. I hate that, it's embarrassing.'

'Why?' I enquire as we make our way down the aisle towards the dried spaghetti.

'It just is. The cashier stares at you like you're a loser and the people in the queue huff and puff. It's humiliating.' I drop three packets of macaroni into the basket.

'There's nothing to be ashamed about, in being poor. I'm studying so I can't work full-time. And you're…' I stop myself. It can't be nice being constantly

28

reminded that you're unemployed. Even with Jimmy's effervescent personality, it must sometimes get to him. He smiles at me.

'You can say it, you know. It's not a dirty word… hang on, yes it is. Unemployed, on the dole, a scrounger, a loafer.' I stare at him. He's smiling but there's a hint of resentment that stain his words. I touch him on the arm.

'It won't always be like this, Jimmy,' I say, offering him some comfort. 'One day you'll look back on these times and laugh—promise.' He purses his lips and thinks for a moment.

'Hmm, maybe. There's more to life than money, right?'

The cashier scans the goods as Jimmy stacks them into a rucksack. He keeps glancing nervously at the till as each item goes through.

'That's nine pounds exactly,' the girl behind the counter says. I smile smugly at Jimmy as I hand over two fivers. He sticks his tongue out at me.

DAVE DEE'S DAY

I throw my leather satchel on top of the metal filing cabinet and flop down into the chair behind my desk. It's just gone 7 am and the newsroom is silent. I like this hour before people arrive, it gives me time to think of the day ahead, before the questions start and the blasted phone starts ringing.

I've given the best years of my life to the Yorkshire Evening Standard and have risen to the position of sub-editor. Next stop—editor, the main man. The paper's fortunes have ebbed and flowed over the years. In the late 1950s, when I started as a junior reporter, we were selling over one and a half million copies a day. The Standard was the biggest regional newspaper in the land, excluding the London Standard. The circulation declined slightly in the sixties then hit a slump in the early seventies, sliding to just over half a million copies a day. The old editor, Tommy James got the elbow and Bulldog became the new editor. He was in his prime then, full of energy and ideas. He turned the fortunes of the paper around and within eighteen months we were back up to the million mark. I hitched my wagon to Bulldog, and he dragged me along for the ride. I owe him a lot. I consider him a friend. He's someone that I respect, but the fact of the matter is, he is now "old-school". He's only got a year or two left before retirement then it will be my turn.

The papers fortunes took another nosedive at the beginning of this year when breakfast TV bounced onto our screens. January 1983 took us all by surprise. No one thought it would take off. Who has time to watch the telly as they're

30

getting ready for work and eating breakfast? Well, the naysayers, including me, were wrong. It has been a huge success and with it came a dramatic drop in circulation, not just for the Standard but for every newspaper.

Our demographic is a broad church. We appeal to the working class, the middle class and dare I say, even the toffs read the paper. Everyone likes to know what's going on in their area. Our readership is ageing though, which is not good. That's why I created a new section in the paper. On the Wednesday edition we now devote a half-page to the local music scene, local bands, big bands, gig reviews and the odd interview. For the Saturday edition, we run a full page of music news and entertainment, in glorious colour. I tried for two pages but Bulldog shot me down. It attracts a younger readership, a readership that if we snare early will keep with us for the next forty years. I explained all this to Bulldog but as I say, he's old school. Anyway, thanks to my efforts with the music section and a few other things I've implemented, the sales have been steadily climbing. We're now just shy of the one million mark again.

Here he comes now, Joe Carmichael, better known to his friends as, Bulldog. His huge frame waddles across the floor as he huffs and puffs. He used to carry his body like a prizefighter, but these days he carries it like a hindrance. He's a big eater and drinker and smokes more than I do. If you want a healthy lifestyle—keep out of the newspaper game.

'Morning, Dave, any breakers?' he asks as he stops at my desk.

'Nah, nothing to talk about. The usual armed robberies, muggings, ram raids—nothing juicy.'

'What we need is another serial killer, like the Ripper. Good grief, that bloke gave us some front pages.' I laugh at his comments.

'Bulldog, the last thing the hardworking folk of Yorkshire need is another serial killer on the prowl.' He chuckles.

'Yeah, I didn't mean it like that. I was thinking of it as a newspaper editor—selling more copies. Right, I'll be tied up all day in meetings with the board. They want me to form a fucking cost-cutting steering committee. All good fun, eh?'

'No problem, Bulldog. I'll run the show.' He pats me on the shoulder.

'You're a good man, Dave. Not sure what I'd do without you.' I watch him as he walks to his frosted office door and disappears inside.

I read through the copy in my in-tray. I pull out my red pen and correct, question and scribble out various sections then place it in my out-tray, ready for the various reporters to collect and rectify. I hear the doors bang open and look up to see young Marky. I glance at the clock on the wall. It's just gone 7:30 am. Marky is a good lad, in fact, another eighteen months from now and he will be my best reporter. He's keen, as sharp as a tack and has a nose for a good story. He also has a caring and gentle side to him, a good bedside manner. He's always early to work and never skives off unless I tell him to. He'll no doubt go through his usual routine.

'Morning, Dave. Bit bloody nippy outside. I'm making myself a brew—you up for one?' I drain the last dregs of tepid tea from my cup and hand it to him.

'Yeah, cheers, Marky. I'll have a coffee.' He stares into the cup and turns his nose up at the stained and tarnished enamel.

'Christ, Dave, when was the last time you cleaned this thing?'

'I never clean it. It makes the tea taste better.' He laughs

'So, what have you got for me today?' he asks, expectantly.

'Law courts,' I mumble as I return to my work.

'Murder case?' he asks with a certain amount of glee.

'Nah, usual,' I reply as I glance at him. His face drops.

'Aw, come on, Dave. When are you going to give me something juicy? I'm sick of writing about missing cats, supermarket robberies and some old lady who's received a telegram from the Queen for her hundredth birthday.' I push back in my chair and stare at him.

'Marky, you're a good lad. I know how you feel. I was once young like you. You've energy and a fire in your belly, you're champing at the bit. Just learn to slow down a bit. It will come to you in time, and when it does, I think you'll be the best reporter this paper has ever seen. Then you'll have the tabloids making offers you can't refuse.'

'Fuck the tabloids! I ain't ever working for them. That's not reporting, that's fairytales and slander. No, I'll be quite happy spending my life at the Standard.'

'Aye, you say that now. Oh, by the way, it's libel, not slander.' He looks a little confused. 'They're both defamation. One written, the other spoken.'

'Yeah, of course—slip of the tongue.' He smiles and makes his way to the kitchen.

There's another thing I like about Marky, he's on my side of the political abyss—he's a Labour man, a socialist. As sub-editor, I have to be impartial, apolitical. The Standard doesn't tell people how to vote on election day as the tabloids do. It doesn't do politics. But, I don't like what's been happening. It used to work quite well. We'd have the Tories in power for a term, then after five years they'd be kicked out and Labour would have a go. Back and forth over the decades. It may not be the most efficient way of leading the country forward but at least it keeps the bastards honest, they can't abuse their power too much. Not now though. The Tories have already had five years in power. They won the last election with a whopping majority, which gives them another five years. Their majority will not be overturned at the next election—unless there's a scandal of epic proportions. That means at least fifteen years in power! That's too long. They can cause a lot of irreversible damage in that time. They've already decimated the steelworks and now they're baiting the miners, looking for a scrap. It's a badly kept secret that they've also been stockpiling coal for the last eighteen months. No, I'm afraid I see dark days ahead. Yes, there's a worldwide recession, but this is a wealthy country and the government is doing nothing to help the working man find work. Four million unemployed and on the rise. If you take away a man's work, you take away his pride. If you take away his hope, all he has left is despair, and desperate men do desperate things.

Marky reappears carrying two steaming cups. He places one down on my desk. He'll have another go—the little bugger is persistent if nothing else.

'Dave, I've been here eighteen months now. I'm ready for some big stories. How am I going to learn if you don't give me a chance?' he pleads. I sip on my coffee and study him.

'Marky, you shouldn't even be here. The Standard gave up on cadetships years ago. We only take on people with a degree behind them now. I had to twist Bulldog's arm to get you this gig. You're keen, I understand that. But, I don't want to spoil the cake by taking it out of the oven too soon. Bide your time, look, listen, learn. You've got the whole of your life ahead of you.' The door bangs open and I watch the figure as it moves, sloth-like across the room. Marky throws a look over his shoulder then turns to me and quietly laughs.

'Here's a man who looks like the rest of his life is behind him,' he whispers. I shake my head at him and resist the urge to smile. John Arnold is our resident photographer, in fact, he's our only full-time shutterbug. The Standard doesn't employ camera guys anymore—part of the cost-cutting. We get most of our shots from a team of freelancers. John is the last of a dying breed—dying been the operative word.

'Morning, Dave, Marky,' he says, dolefully as he takes up his position behind a large table close to my desk.

'Morning, John,' we both reply in unison. He stretches his back and omits a groan.

'Ooh, my bloody lumbago is playing up again. Doc says it's because I spend too much time on my feet.' Some people think John is a hypochondriac, but he's not. He has a lot of real ailments and he doesn't mind telling everyone about them. Most people have learnt to give him a wide berth. Sometimes I feel sorry for the guy—but only sometimes. He was a damn good photographer in his day, but his eyes are shot now and the quality of his work is diminishing fast. He's still got another ten years to go before retirement and we can't sack him as he's in the union—not that I ever would sack him. I'm not sure what we'll do with the blighter in the long term.

'What have you got for me?' he calls out across the room.

'Bookies in Hunslet, got turned over yesterday afternoon. Go get a shot of the manager standing outside. Then, the Lord Mayor is welcoming some overseas dignitaries about midday. Nip up to town hall and capture them shaking hands. Oh, the first job is in Alwoodley, there's a new Tesco supermarket opening up. Some "B" list celebrity is cutting the ribbon. The first fifty shoppers get ten minutes to fill their trolleys for free. Get some smiling faces. I've already got their press release that I'll knock into shape but I want some actual quotes from the shoppers to go with it. I hate this sort of shit, but they've paid for full page ads for the next fortnight.'

'I'm a photographer, not a bloody reporter,' he moans as he rubs his back.

'I could go,' offers Marky, eagerly.

'No. You're at the law courts. John, you need to be adaptable, it's just a couple of quotes, that's all. I'm not asking for an in-depth interview with Prince Phillip.' He nods and totters off towards the kitchen. Marky is still standing at the side of my desk.

'Marky, fuck off and do some work,' I say, without malice. I pick up my red pen, pull another badly typed sheet of copy from my in-tray and set to work.

VIVIENNE'S DAY

The applause finally fades. I stand and make my way to the front of the church hall. I position myself behind the speaker as she grips the wooden podium nervously.

'So, without further ado, may I introduce, Baroness Halliwell to the stand!' she exclaims to the great delight of the meagre audience made up of middle and upper class, dyed in the wool, conservative women. She retires, in a backwards movement, to the fading blue curtains that drape a drab brick wall behind her. I move forward, to the edge of the shallow stage, and begin my speech.

'We all know why we are here today. It's all about the animal sanctuary. Now, some people may call me a hypocrite, after all, I am a meat eater. On our estate, we raise sheep and cattle. I am not a fool. I am well aware of their ultimate demise.

Some people may ask how can I reconcile this fact with my crusade for animal welfare? Well, at Ridley Castle Estate, we treat our animals with care, kindness and respect. They end up on the plate as tender, nutritious meat, free from hormones, free from stress and free from pesticides.

I am not here today to tout my estate's produce. I am here today to hand over a cheque to the North Yorkshire Animal Sanctuary. As you know, my husband is the member of parliament for this area and he has also contributed, considerably, to this cause. We both firmly believe the welfare of animals reflects the human spirit—to care—to help—to respect. I thank you all for attending today and I will be taking tea and biscuits with you all. So, please come up and have a chat. I look forward to meeting you all individually.' I retreat towards the blue curtains as the thirty or so women all rise to their feet and give me a standing ovation—for what, I'm not sure. The speaker retakes her position at the podium.

'I would like to thank Baroness Halliwell for her generous donation of ten thousand pounds to our animal sanctuary.' The ladies clap even harder. I hate these events—they bore me senseless. Don't get me wrong, I do believe in the fair treatment of animals—I want to save them all. I just hate the cabbage-breathing, starchy knicker brigade that is Jeremy's supporter base.

I am standing in a boutique art gallery in Harrogate as the curator pulls the cord that unveils my latest painting. There's a chorus of "oohs and ahs". This is my crowd. The arty, the educated, the bohemians. Once again I make a speech.

'Hello, friends! I shall share a glass of wine with you all, shortly. But, first, let me say that the current painting you are witnessing is part of a trilogy. Yes, I apologise in advance; there's another two in the making—well, in the thinking at least. I will not stand here and tell you what this painting signifies. That is not my job—my job is complete—for the time being. No! It is up to you to interpret this painting as you wish. Abstract means abstract in the fullest sense of the word. What the mind conjures the hand relays.

Please don't ask if you can buy the original. As you know, I never sell my originals, and I'm not sure you could afford them even if I did.' There's a ripple of gentle laughter.

'Prints are being made and will be available in a few weeks. You can place an order today, if you so wish. I'd just like to finish by quoting a great artist, Henry Matisse, "Creativity takes courage". Let us not forget those words. Thank you for being here today.'

##

We reach the climax of our lovemaking and I fall in a heap, exhausted beside him. After a few minutes catching my breath and waiting for my pulse to slow, I roll over and lay my head on his damp chest. He gently strokes my locks.

'Can you stay the day?' he asks, expectantly.

'No, sorry, Garth. I must get back to the castle. The open day is only two days away and we are snowed under. I need to be there to supervise.' He kisses me gently on the crown of my head.

'I thought Victoria was running the show, this time?'

'Yes, she is. However, she still needs supervision. I do worry about her still.'

'Why? She seems like a fine young woman to me.'

'You don't know her like I do. She is without purpose, rudderless. The only time she comes alive is when we do the open days. Then, she is full of fire and brimstone.'

'What she needs is a young man.' I slap him gently on the arm.

'Don't be so sexist. A woman doesn't need a man to be fulfilled. A woman needs a purpose, just like a man does. Anyway, she's so damn picky. She's had plenty of suitors over the years but none of them ever measure up. It never lasts long. Jeremy keeps trying to fix her up, but of course, you know what her relationship is like with her father. If he says night, she will say day.' He chuckles slightly.

'Yes, well, she has your stunning looks, her father's mesmerising blue eyes and, unfortunately, his damned attitude. You should never have married him.'

'Please, Garth, let's not go over this again.'

'Well, Vivienne, I don't understand it. Why don't you just divorce the brute?' I roll away from him and curl into the duvet.

'He's not a brute, he's just stressed—it comes with the job. Anyway, people from my background don't get divorced. We live as a couple, cordially, politely. The men take a mistress—the women—a lover. That's the way it is.'

'You should have married me, back in '61, when I proposed.' I don't reply. Garth is my lover, my friend, my confidant. I am his muse—but—I do not love him, not like I love Jeremy, and always will. That's just the way things are.

'Can we please change the subject?' He rolls into me and continues to stroke my hair.

'Speaking of Victoria, it won't be long now. Is it twenty-two when she becomes the Banduri?'

'No, twenty-three, according to scripture—unless anything should befall me in the meantime. She's still got another eighteen months to go.'

'Is she aware of what is required of her? Does she understand the full importance of being handed the runes?' I sit up sharply and prop my back up with a pillow.

'Of course, she does! She was introduced to the Gathering at age five. She is well aware of her responsibilities and what is expected of her.' I climb out of bed and begin to dress.

'Sorry, just checking. She just seems… well, a little innocent in the ways of the world.' I ignore his comments although I wholeheartedly agree with them. I sit down at the end of the bed as I put my shoes on.

'Vivienne?'

'Yes?'

'Have you thought any more about the photos?' I take a deep sigh. The artistic side of me says yes. I understand that I am the love of Garth's life. I realise that we do not have sex—we *make* love. As an artist, I can understand that he wants to capture that passion on film as photographs, as an artwork. But, for God's sake, my husband is the bloody Home Secretary of the country!

'Garth… I'm not sure it's a good idea. If those photos should ever see the light of day—well, you know the consequences for all of us. It's too risky.' He rises from the bed and pulls his pants on.

39

'Viv, I'm not stupid. I will ensure due diligence. I shall be select in choosing a photographer. He shall be young, naive and have no idea who Baroness Halliwell or Lord Halliwell are. I shall pay him well and insist on the negatives. Please, don't rule it out. Our lovemaking is the purest form of art. We should capture it for posterity. It will only ever be seen by our close circle of like-minded friends.' I stand, pull my hair back into a ponytail and head towards the door.

'I'm sorry, but I must leave.'

'Viv?' he calls out after me. I turn and look at him. 'Don't dismiss it out of hand. Just consider it for a while—that's all I ask.' I smile weakly at him, nod, then exit the door.

JEREMY'S DAY

From my office window, in the Palace Of Westminster, I gaze down into the grey ooze of the River Thames. There's a handful of cruise boats gliding along in both directions, a police boat passes under Tower Bridge and at least a dozen tugs haul their cargos to destinations unknown. The chime of Big Ben, denoting the quarter hour, breaks my trance. I peek at my wristwatch—2:15 pm. It's Monday and I already feel like I've been here a week. It's been a long month and an even longer year. Our election victory in early summer seems a lifetime away, yet, it is only three short months ago.

I place my briefcase on my desk, click open the locks and pull a sheaf of papers from it. I am still hungry... hungry for more power. I was the chief architect behind our stunning political victory and for my efforts, I was offered any position I wanted, apart from PM, of course. For the work that is still ahead of us, there was only one position I could have taken: Her Majesty's Principal Secretary of State for the Home Department, colloquially referred to as the Home Secretary. I believe it is the most powerful office in the land. I am responsible for the safekeeping of this great country of ours. I am in charge of police, immigration, national security, prisons, probation and MI5 answer directly to me. There are other agencies I have at my disposal, the invisible ones that only a handful of people know about.

I speed read through select committee reports, cabinet briefings and recommendations from junior ministers. One recommendation is from Giles

41

Courtney, the rising star of the Tory party. Some tout him as a future leader—over my dead body! Oh, yes, he's young and handsome, he's a natural orator, he has charisma, charm, but the man is a political lightweight. He has no knowledge of the history of this land and what it takes to ensure our enemies, of which there are many, never get the upper hand. But, he is also hungry. I can see it in his eyes. As the old adage goes, keep your enemies close to you. I have taken him under my wing and will encourage and mentor him. It suits my purposes for the moment. At some stage, I will feed him to the hounds. I already have a dossier on him. The damn fool cannot keep his cock inside his trousers. Numerous floozies were paid off before the last election to save his bacon. The PM seems to have a soft spot for him. I also have a soft spot for him—in the mud banks of the River Thames. He comes across as the perfect middle-England family man. A Christian, a teetotaller, righteous and devout. I got sick to death of seeing him trundle out his adoring wife and repulsive looking brats during the campaign. I wonder what the true blue ladies of the Conservative Women's Organisation would think of him if they knew the truth?

As for his report, it is littered with spelling and grammatical errors. His sentences barely make sense and from what I can gather, his whole proposition is preposterous. He is recommending we introduce prohibition! As well as being a lightweight and ignorant of the lessons of history, the man is a nincompoop. I scribble red pen all over his report, circle his typos, add commas here and there and question every statement. At the end, in capital letters, I write, 'GO TO YOUR NEAREST LIBRARY AND READ ABOUT THE RESULT OF PROHIBITION IN THE UNITED STATES!'

Big Ben chimes again. Any moment now and our fiercest attack dog will be here; he's never late. The intercom buzzer sounds. I reach forward and press the button.

'Home Secretary, Sir Duncan Campbell Menzies is here to see you.'

'Thank you, Claire. Just one moment while I finish these papers.' I quickly scribble my signature across two deportation orders, decline a review of an illegal immigration case and deny a request for parole for a notorious gangland murderer from the sixties who has now turned to God. I think he is deluded—doesn't he know—I am now God? I hit the intercom button again.

'Claire, please show Sir Duncan, in.' A few seconds later the door clicks open and my secretary enters with Sir Duncan in tow. I rise from my chair.

'Sir Duncan, what a pleasure to see you. I trust you are keeping well?' Sir Duncan edges towards me and we exchange a warm handshake.

'Yes, never better, Jeremy. I seem to garner more energy the older I get.'

'Good, good! And how's Marjory and the boys?'

'Yes, they're all in fine fettle. How is Vivienne and that adorable daughter of yours?'

'Oh, you know Vivienne, she's either working on some new abstract art painting or raising funds for charity. As for Victoria, well, I see little of her these days. We don't always see eye-to-eye.' Sir Duncan laughs.

'That's because she's like you, a clash of wills. I haven't seen her for many years, but I do recall the last time I met her. She was giving you a hell of a time about some new pony she wanted. You wouldn't budge on the subject and she wouldn't back down.' I'd all but forgotten about the incident. 'Who came out the victor in the end?'

'Ahem, Victoria. Once she gets the bit between her teeth, there's no stopping her,' I laugh, nervously. 'Claire, could you organise tea and biscuits, please.' Claire leaves the room as Sir Duncan sits down in a chair. I take up position behind my desk. 'Duncan, I haven't had a proper chance to thank you for your immense and invaluable support during the election campaign. Without your papers' backing and ferocious attacks on the opposition then I think the result could have been a lot closer than it turned out to be.' Sir Duncan smiles, benevolently.

'Nonsense, Jeremy. The Labour Party is a divided rabble. A bunch of boy scouts could have whipped that lot. With the one hundred and forty seat majority you now have in parliament, you should be able to push through some big-ticket items.'

'Indeed, and that's exactly what we plan to do.'

We sit and exchange our thoughts on various political scenarios that are playing out at the moment and bounce ideas off each other. Claire enters carrying a silver tray adorned with a plate of biscuits, two teacups and a teapot.

'Thank you, Claire. I'll do the honours, that will be all for now.'

'Very good, Home Secretary,' she replies as she glides silently out of the office. I fill the cups with tea.

'So, Jeremy, what's all this about. You didn't call me here so we could gloat over our election victory and drink tea?' I laugh and smile at the old man.

'No, I didn't. It's about Harry Thomas.' Sir Duncan sips on his black tea then picks up a digestive biscuit and nibbles at the side of it, rather like a rabbit would on a lettuce leaf. He wears a furrowed brow.

'Harry Thomas… you mean Red Harry? The Deputy Leader of Greater Manchester City Council?'

'Yes, the one and only.'

'He's a bit low down on the food chain for you to worry about, isn't he?' I sit back in my leather chair and take a drink of tea.

'Well, yes, and no. Yes, Red Harry is nothing but a minor irritant at the moment—a spot fire. But there will be many spot fires over the ensuing months and years. I don't want them to conjoin and turn into a forest fire. There are a lot of changes about to come and people don't like change. There's going to be anger and discord throughout the nation. We don't want some firebrand stirring things up even more. I'm future planning, if you like. Best we get him out of the picture early on in the scene.' Sir Duncan places his cup on the edge of my desk and sighs.

'Jeremy, my tabloids have been banging away at him for eighteen months. The man's a Marxist, a Trotskyite, a fully paid-up member of Militant. We've exposed all this many times, but the damn man openly admits it. He's proud of the fact. He wears the tag, "Red Harry" like a badge of honour. He has a big supporter base in the North West, but apart from that, he's nothing more than a bit player.' Sir Duncan is not hearing me.

'Nevertheless, he has the gift of the gab. He knows how to rally the troops.'

'You don't really see him as a credible threat do you?'

'No, of course not. However, he could pave the way for some unknown player. Someone who is more centrist, more appealing. We need to deal with him and deal with him quickly—nip it in the bud.' Sir Duncan returns to his tea.

'Well, I suppose we could re-hash the stories again, but I'm not sure…' I cut him off.

'No, you've tried that and it's failed. Let's try a different tack.'

'Such as?'

'I was thinking of a femme fatale.' Sir Duncan chuckles, which slightly annoys me.

'Jeremy, we have a dossier a hundred pages thick on the man. He married his childhood sweetheart at age twenty and is happily married with two pre-teen children. It was the first thing my editors looked into. There's nothing that sells papers better than a juicy affair. Unfortunately, Red Harry is clean, nothing, zero. Not so much as looked at another woman. No reports of sexual harassment, no impropriety, no lewd or suggestive comments. I can't see how that angle can work.' I look at my watch. I'm due in the chamber in fifteen minutes and with Sir Duncan being so obtuse, I could be in danger of being late, something the PM frowns upon.

'Come, come, Duncan. An old dog like you must be able to come up with something?' he stares at me blankly. It looks like I will have to hand it to him on a plate. 'What about placing one of your shutterbugs outside a hotel? Red Harry emerges in the morning just as a young, attractive woman walks up to him, flings her arms around his neck and gives him a long passionate kiss?'

'Hmm… a set-up. It could work. But he'd obviously call it out for what it was.'

'A few weeks later the same woman is photographed coming out of town hall. The mystery woman keeps appearing again and again, over several weeks.

Where there's smoke—there's fire. The pressure builds. Then, maybe a few voices emerge from his past with tales of infidelity. At the very least, it would create a huge amount of pressure on him and his wife. He wouldn't have much time for rallying the troops while he's fending off questions about his sex life and the mystery woman. Every man has his breaking point.' Sir Duncan ponders for a moment as though playing the scene out in his head.

'Hmm, possibly. I'll call a meeting of my editors first thing tomorrow morning and run it by them. I don't suppose we've anything to lose. And, if that doesn't work?'

'Well, we'll cross that bridge if and when we come to it. I have plenty more aces up my sleeve.'

'Such as?'

'Oh, you know… connections to the Soviets, misappropriation of funds. We'll weasel him out somehow.' Sir Duncan nods in affirmation.

'Yes. There's always a way. By hook or by crook.'

'Good, good! There's the spirit.' I stand up and hold my hand out. Sir Duncan looks a little taken aback that the meeting has been brought to an abrupt end. We shake hands once more. He ambles slowly as I usher him towards the door.

'So, Jeremy, how's everything else coming along?' I assume he's referring to our master plan of radical reform.

'Everything's falling into place. We've been stockpiling coal at the power stations for the last eighteen months in preparation. The steel union is a shell of its former self and won't have the stomach for a fight, not after all the recent restructuring. McGregor is now drawing up battle plans at the National Coal Board and has been poking and prodding the Miners Union into a fight. Surprisingly, they're showing great restraint at the moment. But, it won't be long before they retaliate—and we'll be ready for them this time.' I open the door for Sir Duncan. He stops and turns to me with an ambiguous smile on his face.

'You know what happened to the last government that picked a fight with the miners?' he drawls, cryptically.

'Only too well, Sir Duncan. I was a Junior Minister at the time. Things are different now. The PM's political will and resolve are unshakeable—as are mine. We will not be bullied and more importantly—we will not be beaten. The die is cast.'

'Hmm, very well, Jeremy. Just remember this though, never catch a tiger by its tail.'

'Unless it's a toothless tiger,' I chortle as I slap him gently on the shoulder.

'Thanks for the tea, Claire,' he says as he departs.

'My pleasure, Sir Duncan,' my secretary replies as the most powerful media mogul in the land strides out of the door and descends along ancient corridors fermented in history.

I'm sitting in the House of Commons as the Honourable Gentleman for Manchester Central asks his turgid and long-winded question.

'I would like to know if the Right Honourable Gentleman for Harrogate and Knaresborough , our glorious Home Secretary, has seen the latest Bureau of Statistic figures on the unemployment rate?' He sneers across the chamber at me. The man is a half-wit, another lightweight, and he looks like his mother may have mated with a gibbon. Before I get the chance to answer, he continues. 'Just in case he missed the figures that were published this morning, let me fill him in.' I'd like to fill him in—bloody imbecile.

'Four million, two hundred and sixty-two thousand, registered unemployed. The figure would be closer to five million if it wasn't for the schemes and scams designed by this government for the sole purpose of reducing the actual figure. Would the Home Secretary care to inform the House what he and his government are actively doing to reduce this horrendous number?' Baying and "here, here" from his own mob of degenerates explodes out in the house. I take my time. I'm a master of this and I know it will be caught by the TV cameras and played around the country on the six o'clock news this evening. I'm never one to miss an opportunity. Sometimes, though, it is just so damn easy. I rise to my feet as my own side cheers. Oh, the theatre, the drama, the games we play. I stare at my opposite number across the floor. What were the Labour Party thinking when they chose Henry Clement to be Shadow Home Secretary? I was actually insulted when he was given the position. Wouldn't you have thought they'd have put the best man at their disposal to take on my might, intellect and political cunning? Oh, well, it's their funeral.

'I would like to thank the Honourable Gentleman for Manchester Central for his question and I will be delighted to answer—even though he will not like the truth. Indeed, he is averse to the truth, rather like an alcoholic is averse to sobriety.' Huge laughs from my own side. It's a bit below the belt, as the moron does have a drinking problem, but, this is politics after all.

'First of all, may I say that I find it a bit rich that he quotes these figures at me when his own local council for Greater Manchester is in a state of chaos and turmoil and on the verge of bankruptcy. Led by "Red Harry", who, by his own admission, is a Marxist, a Trotskyite and a fully paid up member of the Labour Party. Maybe, the Honourable Gentleman could better spend his time helping the good, hard working people of Manchester reclaim their local government rather than slinging misleading figures and numbers at me.' Roars, cheers and the stamping of feet from my side, catcalls and nays from the opposition.

'Answer the question!' shouts a particularly dangerous individual from across the chamber. Why is he dangerous? Because he's articulate, energetic, he can rouse the rabble and worst of all—he's honest. I will deal with Frank Baldwin at a later date.

'Oh, I intend to answer the question! Don't be afraid of that.' I pause for dramatic effect. The house falls silent, momentarily. I begin again.

'1979—the winter of discontent—oh, yes, how could we forget it so soon. Cast your minds back four years. The streets were full of uncollected rubbish as plagues of rats enjoyed a feast. Dead bodies piled up as gravediggers went on strike. Hospitals, picketed by ancillary workers, were left empty—the sick, the old, the dying all turned away. Trains lay idle. Petrol stations around the nation closed

48

their doors as lorry drivers picketed refineries. The miners, the dockers, the steelworkers all on strike. The army was on standby to intervene, an unprecedented move never before witnessed in our democracy.' The roars from opposite are quite deafening now. They don't like a good dose of the truth. I turn to my side and ask the question.

'Who were the perpetrators of this chaos! Who was responsible for bringing this once proud nation to its knees? Who was in charge when the country was on the brink of civil war! WHO! I'll tell you who—the Labour Party!' I yell, pointing my arm at them like a sword. 'A party that is riddled with Soviet sympathisers. A party that has a cancer in its heart! An unruly mob of dangerous malcontents that is unfit to govern!' I do believe that some of my learned colleagues opposite may self-combust at any moment.

'This government inherited a country that was on the verge of collapse, a country at war with itself, a country that was the laughing stock of the world.' A chorus of "here, here" echoes out. 'Since we took charge we have lowered income tax by five per cent, company tax by ten per cent. There are more new business start-ups than there have been in over a decade. We have made a stand against the union bully boys who threaten, harass and intimidate those who are willing to do a fair day's work for a fair day's pay. We are implementing policies that will make this nation great again.

New investment is flooding into the country. We must rebuild from the ground up. The old model that the Labour Party is so fond of is dead. No longer will the taxpayer of Great Britain bail-out inefficient and unproductive industries. No longer will we pour millions into propping up corrupt cronyism. We will become lean, efficient, mobile. We must foster those with zest and initiative, those with energy and vibrant new ideas.' The "here here's" intensify as the opposition becomes ever rowdier. I raise my voice and stick my chest out. 'We must look to the future, not the past. Certain members on the opposite side of this chamber would like to turn this country into a satellite nation of the Soviet Union...' Oh, yes, that's got them going. I pause as the house erupts once more. The newly elected leader of the opposition, Rhys Morgan, is sitting with arms tightly folded and a face like thunder. I can tell what he's thinking. The verbose, ginger-haired, Welsh, fool is having second thoughts about his Shadow Home Secretary. He realises now, that every time he puts a question forward I'm going to rip him to shreds. His incompetent deputy, Roy Pickersgill, sits alongside him, also with arms tightly folded. He shakes his head violently from side to side as he shouts insults at me. His saggy jowls flap as spittle flies from his mouth. And these two clowns were dubbed the "dream-team," only a few months back after their ascension to the leadership. More like the "scream-team".

'Order! Order! Order in the House!' bellows the Speaker. Now for my final flourish. Light the blue touch paper and stand back.

'Thank you, Mr Speaker. This country was once the engine room of the world and with this government, led by the Prime Minister, we intend to make it the engine room of the world once more! We *will* make Britain great again—the future belongs to us!' Bang! The whole house now erupts into a frenzy. From behind me, my side stamp their feet and roar their approval. From opposite, they bay and scream for my blood, pointing fingers at me and waving papers in the air. I remain standing as I turn to my peers and nod sagely, wisely at them. The Prime Minister glances at me, nods and gives me one of those looks that only a PM can give. It is a mixture of respect and pride knowing full well that I have her back, that I am her champion. But, there's also something else there. She understands the game. She realises that one day I will stop being her champion and I shall become her Brutus.

I lean back in my chair as Sir Duncan Campbell Menzies sips on his tea. I pick up a paperknife and hold it between the index fingers of both hands. Sir Duncan chortles.

'Damn fine speech you made today, in the house,' he says, smiling warmly at me.

'Thank you. I can't believe those idiots keep walking right into the same traps. You'd have thought they would have learnt their lesson by now. Can you imagine that buffoon, Henry Clement, as Home Secretary? The mind boggles. I wouldn't trust him to wipe his own backside properly never mind keep the country safe.' Sir Duncan nods at me and crows.

'Yes, there does seem to be a dearth of talent on the opposition side, at the moment. Still, as long as he keeps asking his drab questions it gives you a chance to shine.'

'Yes, I suppose it does. It's strange, but before our election win, I would have given my right arm for a feckless, disorganised, toothless opposition. But, not now. I want to be challenged. I want someone with a great mind, who understands the art of politics and the lessons of history, to duel with. I want the cut and thrust of the chase, someone who can keep me razor sharp.'

'Be careful what you wish for, Jeremy. Count your blessings while you have them.'

'Yes, quite. Right, to business. So, Red Harry—did you discuss him with your editors?' Sir Duncan puts his teacup on a saucer and places it on the side of my desk. I half swivel in my chair and stare out at the cold, grey London streets below. My eyes flit back to focus on the paperknife held between my fingers.

'Yes, yes. It's all in place. Harry Thomas is attending a conference in Brighton, Thursday and Friday of this week. We have a young actress who has been primed. We'll get shots of him as he comes out of his hotel on Friday morning.'

'This young actress, is she safe?'

'Oh, yes. We've used her before. She's on a retainer, she knows which side her bread is buttered. We'll use her again over the next few weeks then we'll pay for her to take a nice long trip to Australia for a few months—let the dust settle.'

'Good, good. So the weekend papers will be full of Red Harry caught with his pants down.'

'Yes. We'll tip off the TV stations on Friday so it makes the evening news; create a bit of momentum. We'll run the story in the Saturday and Sunday editions opposite a piece about Soviet spies and donations from Libya.' I spin back to face him and laugh.

'Sir Duncan, you are a wizard! Subliminal association—I like it.' He leans forward and his expression changes to one of reticence.

'Jeremy, are you sure you want to go through with this?'

'Yes, of course. You have your doubts?' He takes his spectacles off and cleans the lenses on his jumper.

'Well, Harry Thomas could be useful to you later on in the piece.'

'How so?'

'Things will get heated. The miners won't go down without a fight and no doubt they'll get a lot of support from the other unions and a certain amount of public sympathy. They'll see this as the last great battle. If they don't win this one, then they're gone. With their backs to the wall, they could be a formidable opponent. We could skewer Harry Thomas later, as a distraction, when things get tough.'

'You're not getting cold feet are you, Duncan?' He replaces his glasses and shakes his head.

'No, of course not. This is a game of chess and you've got to be thinking five, six moves ahead, that's all. I sometimes get the impression, Jeremy, that you're not playing chess but a game of checkers.' I place the paperknife gently down on my desk.

'I don't think for one minute that this will be the end of Harry Thomas. He'll survive this, but he will be tarnished. We can use him again—later. Anyway, I've got plenty of other distractions that I intend to unleash in the next eighteen months. What have you got on Frank Baldwin?' Sir Duncan looks puzzled as he shakes his head. His saggy jowls swish from side to side.

'Not much. He was briefly a member of the Communist Party when he was a student, but so were most of the Labour Party and even some from your side.'

'Hmm…'

'Why? He's not causing any trouble, and he's not particularly well-liked within his own party.'

'Not yet. He's their future leader. He's biding his time at the moment, waiting.'

'Waiting for what?'

'Waiting until his party ditches its socialist agenda and moves to the centre. He's an opportunist, as all great politicians are. Do a little digging, see if you can unearth a small gold nugget.'

'The Labour Party only elected a new leadership team a few months back—the dream team as they are dubbed. I can't see the party going through more disunity and infighting anytime soon.' Sometimes, Sir Duncan can be very short-sighted.

'No, the Welsh windbag and his slobbering deputy will lead their party to defeat at the next election. That is a certainty. That simpering duo don't have the clout to overturn a hundred and forty seat majority. I'm looking at the election after that—in eight, nine years' time, when I will have been Prime Minister for at least eighteen months. I don't want to lose my first election as PM, that wouldn't look too good on my curriculum vitae. When that election does come around, Frank Baldwin will be leading the opposition and I want plenty of dirt on him.' Sir Duncan rubs his chin thoughtfully.

'Hmm, I see. Well, there was that expenses scandal from a few years ago, but I do believe it was a genuine oversight on his part.'

'Yes, I remember. I don't really want to bring that up. If a witch hunt begins into the abuse of expenses, half of the House Of Commons and three-quarters of the House Of Lords would be embroiled—from all sides.' Sir Duncan laughs.

'Yes, quite. Well, I really must get going. I'll give my people the green light about Red Harry.' He stands and makes his way to the door. I follow him. 'Oh, by the way, Jeremy, there's a hunt on my estate this Sunday—would you care to join us?' I think ahead and remember it's the blasted "Heritage Open Days" at the castle. How I hate those weekends, with commoners and the great unwashed tramping all over my home. Why Vivienne ever signed up for the damn thing, I'll never know. It's not like we need the paltry amount of money it generates.

'Sir Duncan, it would be an honour. It will get me away from the castle. It's one of those blasted open day weekends. Four times a year we throw open our doors to the public so they can shuffle around snooping here and prying there.' Sir Duncan chuckles.

'Yes, Marjory has been badgering me to do the same for years. Says it is "our duty". Blue arses, it's our duty! We'd have to nail everything down. Not sure why you ever agreed to it, Jeremy?'

'I didn't! I expressly forbade it. But, you know Vivienne, she has an egalitarian streak which sometimes worries me. It is her ancestral home, so I didn't have much say in the matter. Anyway, I lock myself away until the clock strikes six and all the buggers have left. What time does the hunt start?'

'10 am, sharp.'

'Hmm, in that case, would you mind awfully if I came down on Saturday night?'

'No, of course not. We can discuss our agenda in more detail. I'll organise dinner for 7 pm, how does that sound?'

'Sounds perfect.'

'Marjory will be delighted to see you. I'll have to tee you up with a partner for the hunt though.'

'Oh, Sir Duncan, if there's any of those damn fool, anti-hunt protestors around, I may have to make myself scarce.'

'Yes, of course, I fully understand. Right, I'll see you on Saturday night.'

I return to my desk and gaze out of the window once more. I'm at the top of my game and I intend to stay here for a very long time. Checkers indeed! I wonder if Sir Duncan realises the dossier of dirt I've got on him? His penchant for buxom call girls dressed in Nazi uniforms is a most peculiar fetish, but, each to their own, I suppose. Yes, I really am reaching the height of my powers. No one in the land can stop me now—no one!

VICTORIA'S DAY

'Victoria? Victoria?' my mother calls out, followed by a gentle tap on my bedroom door.

'Yes, mother, come in, I'm decent.' The door opens and mummy walks in swathed in a fluffy white dressing gown.

'Oh, good. You're up and about. Mrs Beaton is serving breakfast in the Great Hall in thirty minutes. Ready for the big day ahead?'

'Yes!' I reply excitedly. 'A big two days, actually.'

'Indeed. I find it best to take one day at a time though. I enjoy the open days but it is quite wearing.'

'You're getting old, mummy,' I laugh.

'Don't I know it. Right, I'll see you for breakfast in half an hour.' She turns to depart and closes the door gently behind her.

I experience a sudden surge of adrenalin as I think of the day in front of me. I mentally run through the schedule in my head. The first tour begins at 9 am sharp and I am the first tour guide. It lasts approximately one hour, although it can take longer. Mummy takes the second contingent at 9:30 am which then gives me a thirty-minute break before the next tour begins at 10:30 am.

Each circuit of the castle is different. People rarely ask the same questions so it gives me a chance to show my knowledge, which, if I say so myself, is extensive, nearly as good as mummies. The only downside is that father arrived home late last night. Why he bothered to come home at all is beyond me. He's a rare visitor these days, thank God, and he absolutely hates the Heritage Open Days. He'll no doubt be in a bad mood and have a good old grizzle at the breakfast table. I hope he keeps his head down because I will not allow him to spoil it this time.

I quickly shower, do my hair, put my make-up on then stand in front of the mirror as I get ready. I slip into a figure-hugging, navy blue dress, don a pair of comfortable black loafers, throw a set of pearls around my neck and attach a diamond brooch that belonged to my grandmother, to the front of my dress. One last touch is to put on spectacles with clear lenses. It adds a certain gravitas. My whole appearance is one of refined, sensible sophistication, making me look a lot older than my twenty-one years. Well, one must play ones part.

I quickly pull my hair into a bun then open the door, skip along the corridor and descend the sweeping staircase. I make my way through the hallway and creak open the giant front door. It's still a little dark outside but I can tell it's going to be an unusually warm October's day. I can see stallholders erecting tents and laying out their goods. I breathe in the crisp Autumn air. It is perfumed with an invigorating woody mix of decaying leaves and sleepy earth. It is like an elixir and I get a tummy full of butterflies. I close the door and make my way to the Great Hall. As I round the corner, I am greeted with the sound of squeaky trolley wheels.

'Good morning, Lady Victoria.'

'Oh, good morning, Mrs Beaton. Ready for the big day ahead?'

'Yes, Ma'am. I do so enjoy these days. It brings the castle alive to have so many people here.' I open the door to the Great Hall for her as she pushes the breakfast trolley through.

'I know what you mean. I think the Autumn open days are my favourite of all. There's such an atmosphere at this time of year.' Father is sitting at the far end of the room, at the head of the table, of course. He's reading the Financial Times and doesn't stir. Mother sits adjacent to him poring over some notes in front of her. She looks up and smiles at me.

'Victoria, darling, you look wonderful,' she compliments me as she stands up. Mummy is wearing a peach coloured dress akin to my own, also with a throw of pearls around her neck.

'Mummy, that dress really suits you. Elegant, sophisticated, yet also business like.' She laughs and sits back down as Mrs Beaton unloads serving platters with cloches, plates, cutlery and a steaming teapot onto the table. 'Good morning, father,' I say, deliberately more chipper than needs be. I know it will annoy him. He lowers his paper slightly and peers above his horn-rimmed spectacles at me.

'Is it,' he grumbles.

'Yes, it is,' I reply, defiantly, as I take a seat at the table.

'Jeremy, dear, doesn't your daughter look stunning?' He throws me another look.

'Hmm,' is his only retort before returning to the financials.

'Jeremy, will you be dining with us tonight?' asks mother. Father answers but doesn't tear his eyes away from his precious newspaper.

'No. I shall be leaving here at approximately 5 pm.' I smile at my mother and give her the thumbs up. She shoots me a disapproving look in return.

'Oh, that's a rather short visit. What are your plans?' Father, who is impatient at the best of times, folds his paper and throws it down on the table as he grabs a plate, pulls a platter towards him and removes the cloche.

'I've been invited to Sir Duncan's estate for the night. He has a hunt on tomorrow and we also have some business to discuss.' I snort derisively.

'Ah! The English country gentleman. The unspeakable in pursuit of the inedible,' I pronounce loftily, quoting Oscar Wilde. Father doesn't even look at me as he loads his plate with two rashers of bacon, a sausage, a fried egg and two slices of grilled tomato.

'Don't quote that sodomite at me. I'm not in the mood.'

'Jeremy! Not in front of Mrs Beaton!' scolds mother. I try to repress a snigger.

'I'm the master of this house and I'll say whatever I damn well please whenever it damn well suits. I'm sure Mrs Beaton has heard far worse,' he snaps, wearily.

'You may be the master of this house, but I am the matriarch of this estate. May I also remind you I am the daughter of an Earl whereas you are a mere Baron. If I hadn't married below my station, I would now be a Countess instead of a lowly Baroness,' responds mother, caustically but with tongue firmly in cheek. Father bristles at this. It's one of mummy's put-downs that I've heard many times over the years. I can tell it riles him greatly, he has learnt not to take the bait. Oh, I do so love it when father's home—he's such a joy. I help myself to toast, marmalade and a hot cup of tea. I pull my chair forward and kick something soft and fluffy under the table. There's a snippy yelp aired as Molly, the scraggy Yorkshire Terrier, emerges from under the table and eyes me suspiciously.

'Victoria, be more careful,' snaps father as he picks Molly up and places her on his knee. 'There, there, Molly. Did Victoria hurt you,' he coos in a pathetic voice.

'Blasted dog shouldn't even be in here while we are eating,' I reply, angrily.

'Molly is as much a part of this family as you are,' he states, as he breaks a bit of sausage off and feeds it into Molly's mouth. 'Now run along and play, my dear,' he says gently, as he places the mutt on the ground and gives her a pat on the backside.

'Will that be all, ma'am?'

'Yes, thank you, Mrs Beaton. Now, are you sure you've got enough supplies to feed all our visitors?'

'Yes, ma'am. The kitchen staff are preparing sandwiches and cakes as we speak.'

'Very good. Don't worry about dinner for me and Victoria tonight. We'll order a takeaway.'

'Very good, ma'am,' she smiles, before making her way out of the door.

'Don't tell me you're feeding the buggers, as well?' growls father as he munches on his food.

'Yes, of course, we're feeding them. They're paying visitors. If people are handing over five pounds of their hard earned money, then I think it only fair that we provide them with a cup of tea and a cucumber sandwich at the end of the tour,' replies mother.

Father sits in cold silence as mummy and I discuss the day's itinerary.

'So, you're the first cab off the rank at 9 am. Please don't let it drag over too long, Victoria. Last time we got into a terrible muddle once we fell behind schedule.'

'Yes, mother, I'll try. As I've explained, that was a one-off. An American gentleman wouldn't stop bombarding me with questions.'

'Well, remember what I taught you. Walk as you talk.' Father drops his cutlery onto his plate with a clatter and stands up.

'I shall retire to my office for the day to attend to government business. I trust I won't be disturbed by your unruly rabble.' I exchange a mischievous look with my mother as father pours himself a cup of tea then walks towards the door. 'Come, Molly. Remember what I said; keep the riff-raff from my door, otherwise I won't be answerable for my actions.'

'We'll try, dear,' mother calls out after him.

'Tally-ho and give my regards to Mr Fox—if you should catch him,' I add. He stops and peers down his spectacles at me again. We lock eyes briefly before he departs. I burst into laughter.

'Victoria, you're incorrigible. He's in a bad enough mood as it is. Do you have to bait him so?'

'Yes, I'm afraid I do. Why did he even bother coming home at all? He may as well have spent the weekend at Sir Duncan Terrapins?'

'Don't be so rude about Sir Duncan.'

'Well, you've got to admit, he does look like an old gnarled tortoise. If the shoe fits…'

I'm standing on the gravel driveway in front of the grand entrance with a group of about twenty people in front of me—young, old, middle-aged, husbands and wives, partners and lone individuals. I glance at my watch. It's time.

'Ladies and Gentlemen, may I have your attention please!' The throng stop murmuring and give me their undivided attention. 'Before we begin, I'd just like to find out where you're all from,' I announce.

'We're from the United States,' says a rotund man and his wife in unison.

'Excellent! Where exactly?'

'Florida,' comes the man's reply.

'We… er… from Japan,' says a younger man of Oriental appearance, in broken English. He is accompanied by another male and two females.

'And which city do you come from?'

'Fukuoka,'

'Oh dear, I'm not even going to try to repeat that,' I say to muffled giggles. Once I have been around the entire group and determined their origins I look at my watch again.

'Okay, first of all, I would like to offer you a special welcome to my ancestral home—Ridley Castle. My name is Victoria and I will be your guide for the next hour. Please feel free to ask any questions. If you see a room that says, "Private" on it, then please do not enter. This is still a "living" castle and my family's home and as such, there are certain areas that are out of bounds. You are welcome to take photographs at any time, but please, no flashlights. Right, well let's begin, we have a lot to get through. Follow me.' I turn and lead the party up the old granite steps to the main entrance hall.

'Ridley Castle was built in 1309 by Sir William Kilpatrick who saved Edward III from being gored by a wild boar while out hunting. For his bravery, he was knighted and given a large sum of money. The castle has been in the hands of the Kilpatrick family ever since.' We enter the large entrance hall and I talk about the artwork on the wall as the group surrounds me.

'If you care to look behind you at the landscape on the wall. That is a painting by Joseph Turner, the famous landscape painter. He stayed at Ridley Castle in the summer of 1816 as he undertook his Yorkshire Tour. That particular painting is of Hardraw Falls, a local beauty spot.' After a few minutes, I glance over my shoulder and notice the group of Japanese, creeping down the corridor. I call out to them but they either don't hear me or don't understand me.

'Excuse me!' I yell out again. They are getting dangerously close to father's study. I part the crowd and rush down the corridor after them. 'Excuse me!' I'm too late, one of them turns the handle of the door and sticks his head inside.

'Blue blazes! Get out of here! Who the hell do you think you are?' Father's voice booms out. The Japanese look terrified and come scuttling back down the corridor past me, all talking excitedly. Father stands in the corridor and yells.

'Victoria! This is intolerable!'

'I'm sorry, father. I don't think they have a very good grasp of English, so they may not have understood about areas that are out of bounds,' I reply, as calmly as I can.

'I don't care a damn! Keep them away from my office otherwise, I'll boot the buggers out myself!' He's just about to turn when a gruff, male Yorkshire voice calls out.

'Lord Halliwell, can I get your autograph?' Oh, dear. Father turns, slowly. His face is red and his blue eyes bulge from behind his spectacles.

'No! You bloody well can't get my autograph! Who do you think I am? Bloody Mick Jagger!' With that, he turns and slams his office door behind him, the sound echoes violently around the corridor.

'Well, I won't be voting for that bugger come the next election,' grumbles the Yorkshireman. I walk back to the group.

'I do apologise for my father. He is under a lot of strain at the moment and is very busy. Now, follow me—next stop the Great Hall.' I continue to talk as I walk.

'The castle has had a chequered past throughout the years with many famous and dare I say, infamous visitors, staying here. On the 2nd Of July, 1664, the Battle Of Marston Moor was fought between the Royalists and The Parliamentarians, not far from here. The battle was a decisive victory for the Parliamentarians, due in no small part to the commander of their cavalry—Oliver Cromwell. He was slightly wounded during the fighting and billeted in Ridley Castle for a few days to recover. Sir Thomas Kilpatrick was a Royalist and he had to hide in the Old Priory, that used to stand at the back of the castle.'

'What would have happened to Sir Thomas had he been caught?' asks an American.

'He would probably have been beheaded.'

'How important was the battle?' he continues.

'Oh, very important. It changed the course of the civil war. The north of England was now very firmly held by the Parliamentarians. You could say that it led to the evolution of our modern day democracy. It reduced the powers of future kings and queens to interfere in the process of parliament.'

'How many men died?'

'About five thousand, mostly Royalists. Old folklore says that on that day, the rivers ran red with blood.

So, this is the Great Hall, named for obvious reasons…'

##

I'm in the busy kitchen as Mrs Beaton hands me a cup of refreshing tea.

'One down, Lady Victoria, only another three to go,' she offers with a smile. 'How were they?'

'They were very good, attentive and plenty of questions. Only one hiccup, a group of them wandered into father's study.' Mrs Beaton puts her hand to her mouth.

'Oh, no! I thought I heard shouting about an hour ago. How did he take it?'

'How do you think?' I reply as she passes me a slice of ginger cake.

'Not too well, I'd hazard a guess.'

'You'd be right, Mrs Beaton. Anyway, thankfully the old ogre won't be here tomorrow.'

It's just past 5 pm and I am outside with the last tour group of the day. The stallholders are beginning to pack their wares into baskets and place them into various cars and vans. I must admit, my feet are aching and my throat is feeling parched. I point up at the tower.

'The tower is the only remainder of the original castle. A great fire ripped through the building in 1801. Luckily, most of the treasures inside were saved, but the structure was deemed unsound. Work on the new castle began almost immediately and took five years to complete.'

'Who paid for it?' asks an elderly gentleman with a deep Texan drawl.

'It was paid for by Sir William Kilpatrick IV. Now let me get this right— Sir William was the great, great, great, great-grandson of Sir William Kilpatrick I.'

'Where did he get his money from?' asks the wife of the Texan.

'Sir William was an astute businessman and didn't miss his chance when the industrial revolution began in the 1750s. He already owned many coal mines and when the steam engine was invented he invested heavily in the new technology. With the aid of the steam engine, he could pump water from flooded mines and so extract even more coal, which in turn was burnt by steam engines to produce more energy. He then invested in steel and the burgeoning railways. Steel is heavy and needed to be transported by railway and as we all know, trains run on railway lines made of steel. They also required coal to create the steam to power them. He created a self-fulfilling money loop which made him the equivalent of a billionaire today.'

'Bet he didn't pay his workers much,' grizzles a Liverpudlian man.

'On the contrary. His workers were some of the highest paid in the land. Not only that, but he built many small towns around Yorkshire and Lancashire where workers could live rent free. He built hospitals and schools so the worker's children would receive an education. He paid women the same rate as men, which was unheard of, and still doesn't happen to this day. He ensured clean drinking water, built municipal bathhouses and gave land for allotments so people could grow their own food. He was ahead of his time. In fact, if you worked for the Kilpatrick Family you were considered very lucky indeed.

This fostered in the workforce a sense of loyalty and wellbeing. The productivity of the various Kilpatrick businesses was unsurpassed throughout Europe—probably the world. He reduced the working week to five and a half days; gave the workers a week off at Christmas and a week during summer, on full wages. He took a small amount of their weekly wage and invested it in stocks and shares. When a worker was no longer able to work, due to ill health or old age, they were paid a weekly amount from this investment fund—rather like a pension of today. He also had a fund to help with funeral costs. Which just goes to prove that you can create wealth for yourself and look after your workers at the same time. The two things are not mutual opposites.' I'm not sure it was what my Liverpudlian friend was hoping to hear.

I look back towards the main entrance and notice father marching down the steps. He has an overnight bag slung over his shoulder, a briefcase in one hand and Molly tucked under his right arm. His Chauffeur leaps from the Range Rover and opens the boot as father deposits his bags in the back. The driver slams shut the boot as father climbs into the passenger seat and places Molly on his lap. The car sets off at a sedate pace along the gravel driveway. There's a group of five or six tourists standing in the path of the car with their backs to it as it approaches. I see father lean across to the driver's side and blare the horn three times. The group of tourists jump in the air, startled, and quickly move to the side of the driveway. As the vehicle passes, father sticks his head out of the window and yells at them.

'Get out of the way you damn fools! Are you trying to get yourselves killed!' My tour group all turn to witness the inexcusable scene.

'Who's that?' one of them asks.

'Lord bleeding Halliwell,' say the Liverpudlian with a sneer.

'Come, come,' I command. 'We've still got a lot to get through.'

I guide them around to the rear of the castle into the large courtyard with the lake in the background. I explain how the lake was built, point to a spot of rubble where the Old Priory used to be, then finish up. As I'm giving my closing address, I notice one of the group peering intently at the rectangular glass case mounted on an ancient stone plinth.

'Victoria?' the man calls out, in a broad Yorkshire accent. 'What's this stone carving all about?' I wander over to him as the group follow behind me.

'That is an ancient Gaelic artefact of the Goddess Morrigan.'

'Morri who?' he says, sticking his nose to the glass.

'Morrigan,' I reiterate. 'The Phantom Queen, The Great Queen, or depending on which scholar you read, The Faery Queen. She was revered and feared in Celtic mythology.'

'Why?' he queries, squinting at the object.

'She was the Queen of war, of life and death—of destiny. Legend has it she could foretell people's deaths and by what means. She was also a shape-shifter.'

'A shape-shifter? What the 'ells a bloody shape-shifter?'

'She could take many forms, not just human. She could appear as a raven, a cow, an eel. The raven signifies death. Probably because after fierce battles flocks of ravens would descend to feast upon the fallen.' The grizzled old man looks at me.

'Fairy tales, then,' he chuckles. I stare at him intently.

'Sorry, but I forgot your name?' I ask politely.

'Brendan, Brendan Watson,' he replies, as the smile dissipates from his face.

'Well, Mr Watson, some may call them fairy tales others would call them cautionary tales. I wouldn't mock the Morrigan, lest something dreadful befall you.' He looks back at the stone relic.

'I tell you what, she's a big-chested lass,' he sniggers.

'How very observant of you, Mr Watson. Indeed, she has a very large pair of breasts—obviously carved by a man.' All the women around me laugh and Brendan looks a little embarrassed.

'What's it worth?' he asks.

'It is invaluable, priceless.'

'Aren't you worried it might get stolen?'

'Whoever stole the Morrigan, would soon bring her back, I can assure you of that, Mr Watson. Right, ladies and gentlemen. I hope you enjoyed the tour and please visit us again sometime. We are open to the public four times a year. If you'd care to follow me into the Great Hall, I have sandwiches and refreshments awaiting you.'

I'm sitting with mother in our cosy TV room eating takeaway Chinese food on my knee.

'I'm simply exhausted,' complains mother.

'Me too,' I concur. 'I'm going to eat this, then take a long, luxuriating bath and get an early night.' I look at the clock on the mantelpiece. It's nearly 9 pm.

'Yes, well, I intend to watch the news then go straight to bed myself.' She flicks the remote control and the TV flickers to life as the theme tune to the BBC news flows from the speaker. The familiar face of the newsreader emerges.

'An IRA bomb defused in Birmingham. CND march attracts largest crowd ever. A huge earthquake in eastern Turkey, a thousand feared dead. But first, to our top story.

The Deputy Leader of Greater Manchester City Council, Harry Thomas, has today fended off questions about his relationship with a young woman. The firebrand deputy, who is a self-confessed member of the far-left Marxist group, "Militant", was pictured kissing the woman as he left his hotel in Brighton this morning.' The screen cuts from the newsreader to the front pages of the tabloid press. It shows a woman with long blonde hair, wearing sunglasses, with her arms wrapped around a man's neck, her lips firmly planted on his.

'This will cheer your father up,' says mother with little enthusiasm.

'Why?' I mumble through a mouthful of rice.

'He loathes the man. Calls him a Marxist pot-stirrer.'

'Ha! Father thinks anyone who is slightly left of Hitler is a Marxist pot-stirrer,' I snort. The TV screen now jumps to a slurry of reporters and cameramen following Harry Thomas down the road.

'Mr Thomas, how long has this affair been going on?'

'Harry? Harry? What has your wife had to say about these revelations of your affair with a woman half your age?'

'What do you think your fellow councillors will make of this disclosure?'

'Is this the end of Red Harry? Do you plan to resign, Mr Thomas?' The poor man is being hounded to death and I feel quite sorry for him.

'He's very dapper for a so-called Marxist?' I observe.

'They're not all dressed in donkey jackets and hobnailed boots, dear. But, I must admit, he is attractive,' replies mother.

'I don't see what the big deal is. Don't all married couples have affairs?'

'Victoria! Don't be so cynical,' she replies sternly.

'Well, it's true. Daddy has his mistress and you have Garth.'

'Victoria! Really! I don't want that cheap little floozy's name brought up in this hallowed house!'

'I didn't bring her name up. I called her his mistress,' I contend.

'And another thing—Garth and I are just close friends. We are not lovers. I don't know where you get such ideas from.'

'Oh, stop the pretence, mother. I've seen you two together. He's besotted with you. He's also quite attractive, for an older man. Not too dissimilar in looks to Red Harry.' I focus back on the TV screen. Red Harry stops to face his inquisitors.

'I will be taking legal action against the Menzies tabloids for this scurrilous set-up. For that is what it is! I do not know the young lady in question. To the best of my knowledge, I have never met her before. This was a well-rehearsed and choreographed sting. My wife stands by me and I will not be resigning as Deputy Leader Of Greater Manchester City Council—I have done nothing wrong. This is simply a diversion tactic from the powers above to deflect attention away from the parlous state of the nation and the mass unemployment we are undergoing due to government policy and inaction. I have no further comment to make.'

'Now to other news. A bomb warning was issued today in…' The TV goes blank as mother hits the remote control "off" button.

'He's right,' I state.

'What do you mean?'

'The photograph. She has her arms draped around his neck. Lips locked on his, one leg kicked back in the air—yet, he has his arms rigidly straight down by his sides, almost like he's frozen. He wasn't enjoying the experience. If it were his mistress, don't you think he'd be a bit more emotive in his body language?'

'Not necessarily,' she yawns. 'Right, that's me done for the day. I'm hitting the sack. Thanks for your help today, Victoria. I really couldn't do it without you.' I smile at her.

'Don't be silly. I love it, I really do. It gives me a purpose.' She walks over to me and strokes my hair. 'Oh, mummy, I forgot to tell you a funny thing about today. I was wrapping up the last of my tours and one rather gruff old Yorkshireman became engrossed in the Morrigan. He wasn't particularly interested in the history or its significance. He was more fascinated with the size of her breasts.' Mummy chuckles.

'Men,' she simply replies before bending and kissing me on the cheek.

'Night, mother,' I say as she heads out of the door.

'Goodnight, darling. We'll do it all again, tomorrow.'

JIMMY'S NIGHT

There's a blare of a horn. I pull the curtains back and stare out into the front garden. Macca's van is parked in the driveway. I can't make out any faces as it's already dark.

'Sofe! Are you ready, they're here?' I yell out.

'Nearly!' comes her disembodied reply. I adjust my hair in the mirror, spray some deodorant under my armpits, pull on a black Fred Perry then grab my jacket and camera. I skip down the steps into the hallway.

'Come on, girl! You can't keep future superstars waiting.'

'Superstars, my arse,' comes her reply. Her door opens and she steps out into the hallway. 'Well, how do I look?' She looks bloody good, as she always does.

'You'll do,' I reply as I usher her towards the front door.

'Oh, thanks for your resounding endorsement. You certainly know how to flatter a girl,' she pouts. I pull the door shut behind us and we make our way to the van. There's a large logo on the side. It is of a clenched fist holding a lightning bolt. Above it are the sign-written words, "Macca's Delivery Services". Underneath the logo, is a statement, "Faster Than Lightning". Macca sticks his head out of the driver's window.

'Come on, you two. Get a move on. We're already running late. You know what Iris is like.' I give him the thumbs up and we both scoot around to the passenger side. I open the door.

'Gerry, Jonesy, how's it going?' I say to my mates who are looking nice and cosy in their seats as reggae music quietly plays in the background.

'Yeah, good, Jimmy. Come on, hop in the back,' says Gerry.

'Hang on, we have a lady in our presence. Are one of you going to give up your seat for her?' I say.

'Lady?' says Jonesy. 'I don't see a lady, do you, Gerry?' He looks around as though Sofe is invisible.

'Nah, I can't see a lady. I can see Jimmy and Sofe but definitely no lady.'

'Fucking smartarses,' scoffs Sofe.

'Sorry, Sofe,' I say as I slam shut the passenger door. 'I did try.'

'That's alright, Jimmy. I don't want to sit with those dickheads anyway,' she replies, loud enough so they'll hear. A chorus of "oohs" emanates from the front. I open the back doors of the transit van and clamber in. I offer Sofe my hand and pull her up. The van is half full with drum cases, amps and guitars. I take up position on a large flight case and Sofe sits down on the bass drum case.

'Oi, get you fat arse off the fucking drums! You'll break the skins,' bellows Jonesy. Sofe rolls her eyes and mutters, "wanker" under her breath. Macca slams the van into reverse and shoots backwards at an alarming rate. He hits the brakes and I instinctively grab onto Sofe so she doesn't go flying out of the doors.

'Oh, I forgot to mention, Macca is the worst driver in the world,' I inform Sofe.

'Great,' she sulks as she takes up position opposite me on another flight case then grabs onto a strap that hangs down from the van roof. The music is turned up to deafening proportions as we fly down the road.

I watch nervously from the back as Macca overtakes three cars in a row, then veers violently back to the left-hand side of the road missing an oncoming bus by inches. Gerry and Jonesy let out a collective "Whoa!"

'He's a bleeding nutter!' exclaims Sofe.

'Trust me, this is him being sedate. Wait until the journey home, once he's got a few beers in him.' Sofe looks horrified.

'If he gets pulled over he could lose his licence; then he'd be out of a job.'

'His license is already suspended,' I chuckle. Sofe shakes her head in disbelief. There's a chorus of angry blasts from horns and the squeal of car tyres as Macca speeds through a red light.

'Jesus!' says Sofe. 'What was that thesis called, I was going to write about you?'

'Delusion, Denial and Overconfidence in Teenagers,' I retort. 'Except Macca is no teenager. He's an old fart. Turned twenty-two last month.'

We race down a slip road that merges with the inner ring road in the heart of the city. The speed limit signifies 50 mph but a quick glance at the speedometer says we are nearly touching 90 mph. The van slides gracefully into the traffic and moves immediately into the outside lane. There's a car, obeying the speed limit, which slows Macca down and infuriates him. He blares the horn, once, twice, thrice.

'Come on, grandad! Get out of the fucking way!' he yells, hitting the horn again. The car moves across and Macca hits the accelerator hard.

'Plods, dead ahead!' I hear Jonesy shout.

'Yep, spotted them,' says Macca as he hits the brakes. Sofe flies forward and I hold out my arms and catch her. Her lips are nearly touching mine as I smile at her. I expect her to push herself away from me… roughly… but she doesn't. There's something that flashes across her eyes and she lingers longer than she should.

'Thank you,' she whispers quietly. Once we are safely past the cop car, Macca resumes normal service. After another ten minutes in the van and numerous close calls and near misses we are all laughing like demented hyenas. It's the sort of laughter you get when you're on a scary rollercoaster ride. A mixture of terror and unbridled exuberance. Even Sofe has tears of laughter streaming down her face now.

I can see the Granary fast approaching and as we near the front doors, Macca slams on the brakes so hard that the van skids to a halt overshooting the entrance. He quickly slams it into reverse, does a wheel spin, mounts the pavement, then thankfully, turns the engine off. There are audible gasps of relief from all aboard, apart from Macca who has already jumped from the van. I tentatively open the back doors and get out. I hold my arm out for Sofe to hold onto as she jumps from the back. Macca marches up to the red double doors of the Granary. They are firmly shut and there's no sign of life. He bangs hard on them five times whilst shouting out,

'Police! Open up, this is a raid!' he turns and grins at Gerry and Jonesy as they stretch their bodies after escaping the harrowing ride. Macca bangs violently, again, this time shouting,

'Okay, boys! Get the battering ram and be ready with the teargas!'

'Daft bastard,' smiles Sofe. There's a clank of bolts before the doors are rudely thrown open. Iris emerges, looking less than impressed.

To the untrained eye, she could be anyone's doting old granny. Diminutive, grey haired, half-moon glasses with a red crocheted shawl around her shoulders. Don't be fooled by appearances. Iris is one of the canniest businesswomen going around. She took over the dilapidated and abandoned old grain store about five years ago and turned it into one of the busiest nightclubs in Leeds. Not only that, but it is the coolest place to be seen.

'What's all this commotion! What is this about the police!' she yells in her eastern European accent. Macca smiles at her then picks her up and spins her around before dumping her back on the ground.

'Good to see you, Iris. Thanks for the gig. We won't let you down,' he says. Iris begins slapping him around the arms and shoulders.

'You great big ape! You're late! Come, come, hurry up!'

We begin unloading the gear and deposit it in the gloomy entrance of the Granary.

'Right, Iris, ' begins Macca. 'How much did you say you were paying us?'

'You know very well how much I'm paying you,' replies Iris, sternly.

'One fifty, wasn't it?' says Macca.

'That's right. Have you a problem with that?'

'No, not at all,' Macca laughs. 'Of course, we'll need another thirty quid for petrol money and a rider.'

'Ha!' Iris scoffs. 'There'll be no petrol money and no rider. Who do you think you are? Big shots?'

'What's a rider?' Sofe whispers to me.

'It's food and drinks provided backstage for the band by the promoter—in this case, Iris.'

'Okay, boys, let's load the gear back into the van.' We all pick up various pieces of equipment and make our way back outside. Macca opens the back doors of the van and begins to manoeuvre a wheeled flight case into position. Iris follows behind.

'I will give you ten pounds for petrol money and one crate of Bulgarian beer. That is my final offer,' she states in a cross manner. Macca turns and studies her for a moment.

'Tell you what, twenty quid petrol money and two crates of beer—but not that Bulgarian crap. It tastes like witches piss.'

'Bulgarian beer is the finest in the world,' states Iris with a look of disbelief.

'No, it's not. It's the worst beer in the world. We want some good shit, like Heineken or Stella,' Macca says. Iris shakes her head.

'You Hipnotikz always give me trouble. I don't know why I bother with you,' she mumbles, unhappily.

'Because, Iris, we're the best band in Leeds and your main act is not turning up tonight and you need someone to keep the punters entertained. Without us, you'll be standing here all night apologising and handing out five pound notes as refunds. I know you, you don't like to part with your cash. You need us more than we need you right now. Twenty quid and two crates of Heineken,' he repeats. Iris eyes him coldly for a moment.

'Fifteen for petrol, and a crate and a half of Budweiser. That's my final offer,' she says, folding her arms as she pulls a mean expression. Macca smiles as he walks up to her.

'Okay, deal.' He spits into his palm and holds it out. Iris spits into hers and they shake on it. After they relinquish their grips Iris bursts out laughing.

'Oh, Macca, you're too easy. You need to smarten up. I was expecting to pay you fifty for petrol and three crates of beer of your choosing.' She slaps him gently across the cheek three times. She turns and walks back inside chuckling to herself. Jonesy and Gerry burst out laughing.

'Jeez, Macca, she played you like a fiddle,' says Gerry. Macca smiles.

'She's a fucking wily old bird, that one.'

##

The band are going through their soundcheck as me and Sofe chat with Iris.

'So, Jimmy, why have I not seen you for so long?' she asks.

'I'm perpetually skint,' I reply. She rolls her eyes heavenward.

'Jimmy, you could get a job if you really tried.' Here we go, she always gives me this lecture.

'Iris, I do try. I'm always applying for the few jobs that are advertised. I trail around all the record and music shops weekly asking the managers if they have any work for me. Times are tough, Iris, bloody tough.' I sip on my Budweiser as she begins counting out money that she puts into a float tin. 'How about you give me a job here?' I try my luck, again. She peers above her spectacles at me.

'What as? You wouldn't make a good bouncer and all my bar staff I've had for years. I can't just get rid of one of them to give you a job. If one should leave, I'll give you a call.'

'See?' I reply. She finishes counting out the notes and coins, shuts the lid on the little metal box, then locks it. She looks at Sofe who is also gently sipping on a beer.

'You have a very pretty girlfriend. You should marry her before someone else does,' she advises. Sofe snorts out a stream of beer from her nose. 'Did I say something funny?' asks Iris, looking annoyed.

'Oh, we're not... you know,' begins Sofe, pointing back and forth between herself and me.

'You're not what?' asks Iris.

'We're not boyfriend and girlfriend,' Sofe explains. Iris looks puzzled.

'Why not? You are a beautiful looking girl and Jimmy is young and handsome. If I were your age I would be getting Jimmy into the sack as quickly as possible.' Now it's my turn to snort beer out of my nose. Sofe giggles. 'What is the problem? Are you a lesbian?' I'll give Iris one thing—she doesn't mince her words.

'No. No, I'm not a lesbian. Although you're not the first to ask that question. Me and Jimmy are flatmates. We share a house together. I'm a student.' Iris pulls her shawl tightly around her shoulders.

'And what has that got to do with anything? You share a house together, why not share a bed together?'

'It's not like that. We're just mates... I suppose,' Sofe is now looking decidedly embarrassed. Iris whistles through her teeth and tuts.

76

'Yi, yi, yi, yi, yi! What is that old English expression… youth is wasted on the young.' The door bangs open as Marky walks in.

'Welcome, Blisters!' I call out to him. 'Funny you should turn up after all the hard work is done.' He grins at me and holds out a fist.

'Comrade,' he says as I reciprocate. He turns to Sofe, 'Sister,' he states as Sofe gives him a half-hearted fist bump. He looks at Iris and holds out his fist to her, 'Grandma,' he smiles. Iris clips him around the head.

'Don't call me grandma! And enough with the comrade shizen. You forget that I lived under communist rule for most of my life. It was not good. In fact, it was terrible. You should go to Bulgaria and live there for a year, Marky. It would soon stop your notions of a communist utopia.'

'Calm down, Iris, calm down,' Marky chuckles.

'That will be five pounds if you've come to see the band,' she says holding out her hand. Marky spreads his arms out.

'Iris, I'm with the band!' he exclaims. Iris shakes her head.

'A three-piece band that has three roadies? Rather extravagant for a band with no record deal, don't you think?'

'Who said anything about a roadie. No, I'm above that lowly station. I am the Hipnotikz guru. Think of me like the Maharishi to the Beatles. I give them mental sustenance, I am their moral compass.' Macca's voice booms out over the club's PA system.

'Oi, Marky, you wanker, get me a beer will you. There's a crate backstage.'

There's a large crowd that turns up and a lot of them are bloody pissed off that the band they came to see are not playing. Iris hands out two ticket stubs that entitle each customer to two bottles of beer as compensation. I'm assuming it will be Bulgarian beer. There's a handful of people who insist on their money back but Iris won't budge. The best she offers is a signed chitty to the value of five pounds that they can use in the future. See? I said she was a canny businesswoman. A couple of lads start to kick up a storm but they are soon silenced when big Mal approaches. Mal is the Geordie bouncer who has been here for years. He speaks gently most of the time unless he gets angry. I've seen him in action and he fights like a Trojan. With Mal, you get three for the price of one. He has a quiet word with the lads and they slink off towards the bar cursing under their breath. Mal spots me and makes a beeline towards me.

'Shit,' I whisper.

'What's wrong?' asks Sofe.

'It's Mal, he's heading this way.' Sofe glances over her shoulder.

'So what? I thought you two got on well together?'

'We do, but Mal would like to take things further.'

'You mean he's gay?'

'Yes. And I've spotted his schlong whenever he follows me into the gents. It's like a baby's arm.'

'Don't knock it until you've tried it,' she giggles. I sigh and take a sip of beer.

'There's no way I'll be trying "it". I wouldn't sit down for a week. Pretend to be my girlfriend—throw him off the scent.'

'Jimmy, Jimmy, Jimmy—where have you been all my life? I've been worried about you,' Mal laughs as he places his large mitt on my left shoulder and begins to massage it.

'Hi, Mal. Yeah, I've been keeping a low profile. I'm sick of the paparazzi following me around everywhere.' He smiles and turns to Sofe.

'And who do we have here?'

'Mal, this is Sofe, my, ahem, girlfriend. Sofe this is Mal.' He eyes me suspiciously as he shakes hands with Sofe.

'So, girlfriend, eh? How long you two been going together?' As I say "a few weeks" Sofe blurts out, at the same time, "eighteen months". There's an awkward moment before Sofe leans in and kisses me gently on the lips.

'Here, hold this Jimmy. I need to powder my nose,' she says handing me her bottle of beer. There's silence as we both watch her disappear into the crowd.

'So, which is it? A few weeks or eighteen months?'

'It's a few weeks. What Sofe meant is that we've actually known each other for eighteen months.' He nods, silently, doubtfully, with a mean expression on his face. I offer him a weak smile and he chuckles.

'Well, pretty boy, when you see the light, you know where to find me.' He squeezes my shoulder again and turns to head back to the main entrance.

The Hipnotikz play for forty-five minutes, take a half-hour break then return to the stage again for the final hour. I've watched them a hundred times before, and there is never a bad gig, but tonight they are blisteringly good. The crowd was cool and standoffish at first, but by the time they begin their second set, they come alive. The light show is great, the sound is crystal clear and Macca prowls the stage like some acclaimed Shakespearean actor as Jonesy and Gerry provide the sublime rhythm section.

I'm standing in the wings behind them. I've already got some good shots from the front of the stage, but now I want to get some of them from this position. There's a thin film of dry ice that hangs in the air. The crowd jump up and down in unison as steam rises from the mass of bodies. I get three good shots of the scene. I look across the stage into the other wing. Sofe is leaning against a wall peering out at the band and crowd. She looks wistful, almost sad. I focus the camera in on her and capture the poignant moment forever. She notices the flash and turns to me. She's almost expressionless now. She closes her eyes. Her breasts rise and fall. I get another shot of her. She's been acting peculiar all night. One minute she's happy and exuberant, then the next minute she's quiet, reflective. I know she can be moody, but to swing from high to low and back again in the space of a few minutes seems quite odd to me.

By the time we have packed up all the gear and loaded it into the van, the last of the crowd has been rounded up by Mal and pushed out of the door. We all hang back and chat with Iris, Mal and Nelson for a good hour, drinking beer and having a laugh. We then head to the curry house where Macca insists on paying for all the curries and I make sure I fill up big time.

I'm not sure how many beers Macca has drunk tonight, but for some reason, he drives me and Sofe back home at a relatively normal pace. As we get out of the van he leans out of the window and thrusts a twenty quid note towards me.

'Here, Jimmy, Sofe, take this,' he shouts.

'Nah, don't be daft, Macca. You've already given us free beer and paid for our meal. That's more than enough,' I explain.

'No, I mean it… take it. Old Iris did end up giving us fifty for the petrol money, after all, so we're well out in front. It's been a good night, now take it!' he commands. I shake my head.

'No!' I insist. Sofe walks over and grabs the note from Macca's hand.

'Thanks, Macca—it is appreciated, and thanks for a great night.' She turns and walks to the front door. Macca is already reversing hard back down the driveway. I wave at the boys who all wave back.

'Marky, I'll see you Thursday lunchtime in Tossers!' I shout out after the van. Marky sticks a clenched fist out of the window and shouts,

'Comrade!' I watch for a few moments until the van slides out of view. I love those boys.

I follow Sofe into the kitchen as she flicks the kettle on.

'Tea?' she asks. I nod. 'Why didn't you take the money?' I pull a chair out from under the table and sit down.

'We got a free night out. That's enough. They're my mates. I don't want to take advantage.' She drops fresh tea bags into two cups and stares at me.

'Jimmy…' I assume I'm going to get a lecture about money. The pause is so long I think she may have forgotten what it was she was going to say. I blink and begin to tap the table with a finger. 'Jimmy… I… think…' She pauses once more and averts her gaze from mine. She's acting weird again, maybe it's the booze. 'Jimmy… it's just… what I mean to say, is that…'

'What?' I ask, exasperated by her reticence. She seems to snap from her reverie as the kettle clicks off.

'If people offer you money in return for your help, well, then make sure you take it. We need it more than they do.' She turns and pours boiling water into the cups.

'Right… okay,' I reply, nonplussed. I've no idea what all that was about.

She places the two cups on the tiny, well-worn kitchen table, pulls out a chair and sits. She grips her mug of tea with both hands, bends forward and sips.

'Ah! Fresh tea! That tastes good,' she states. We sit in silence for a few seconds.

'What's wrong, Sofe?' I enquire. She pushes back in her chair and stares at me.

'Are you blind?' she retorts.

'Maybe.'

'Yes, you are. We have nothing. We scratch an existence from day-to-day. Twenty quid—no…five quid is like we've hit the jackpot! This house is falling apart; the rent is too high; the place is infested with woodlice, cockroaches, mice. You score a few blocks of cheese for free and you think you're a millionaire.'

'I told you earlier, I am a millionaire,' I reply with a cocky smile. She buries her face in her palms.

'Oh Jimmy, stop,' she wails.

'Stop what?'

'Stop with the façade of false positivity,' she mumbles as tears begin to roll down her cheeks. I take a long, slow drink of my brew.

81

'It's not a façade,' I reply gently. She sniffs. 'It's a choice. Every morning when I wake up I have a choice. Do I get out of bed and look at my life as it really is? I have no future, I have no money, no prospects—not just now, but for years ahead. As my dad would have said, "I don't have a pot to piss in."

I know I fucked up at school, I didn't listen, I didn't study… but that's not the cause of my problems. There's fucking architects and scientists queuing up at the dole office.

Do I give up? Do I throw the towel in? No! I get on with it. I eat whatever comes my way. I take free pints off my mates. I listen to my music. I go and watch local bands. I take photographs of life—I keep on keeping on—surviving, living. There is beauty, everywhere, if you only open your eyes.

Sofe, I don't have any other fucking choice. The alternative doesn't bear thinking about. You can call it a façade, but it's not. It's who I am. I'm Jimmy, happy-go-lucky Jimmy. I give two fingers to the world and all who sail in her—and one day—one day… maybe things will change.'

'Sorry,' is her only reply. I grab her hand.

'Hey Sofe, how many times have I told you, it won't always be like this. Cheer up! A year from now you will be a fully-fledged psychologist with a degree stuck in your back pocket. The Hipnotikz will be world-famous and selling a gazillion albums. Marky will be the most feared reporter in the land. Three years from now, you'll have your own practice, be married to a wonderful man and living in your dream home—without mice or woodlice.' She rubs the tears from her cheek with the back of her hand then fixes me with a sad expression.

'And where will you be?'

'Me? I'll still be sitting here. I ain't going nowhere. You can come back and visit whenever you like. The cockroaches will be glad to see you.' She giggles slightly, then sniffs.

'You idiot. Jimmy… I… '

'Yes?'

'Jimmy... I'm going to bed.' She takes a gulp of tea, stands and makes her way out of the room. She comes to a halt as she leaves the kitchen. She turns to me. 'Jim, make something happen—for yourself—and be quick.' I stare thoughtfully at her as she disappears into her room and closes the door. Her words bounce around my head like a pinball. I pull the camera from around my neck and place it on the table in front of me.

'Yeah Jimmy—make something happen—and be quick,' I murmur to myself. 'But *what?*'

THE END... for now

Would you like to read the next book in this series?

THE SOUL LOVE SERIES

I hope you enjoyed this prequel in the Soul Love Series. It gives you a little taster of the characters that star in book 1 - **Love Is The Goal,** where the story really starts. Find out what happens to Jimmy and his pals as the country becomes ever more divisive and violent. Follow Victoria's journey from loveless isolation to happiness, as she begins to bloom and become a formidable force in her own right. I have an excerpt below to whet your appetite.

You can purchase the ebook of Love Is The Goal via this link.

Soul Love: Prequel – Out Now

Love Is The Goal: Book 1 – Out Now

Love On The Roll: Book 2 – December 2019

Love Of The Coal: Book 3 – 2020

Love In The Soul: Book 4 – 2020

All books will be available in paperback and ebook.

 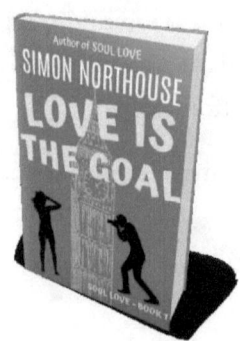

Join My Mailing List

If you would like to receive an email reminder when each book is released, then sign up to my irreverent and amusing monthly newsletter, "Discombobulated". Not only will it entertain you, but I also give my subscribers some free or heavily discounted "goodies" throughout the year.

The link below will take you to my website sign-up page, and I'll also gift you a couple of free books.

http://www.snorthouse.com/home-page/newsletter-sign-up/

REVIEWS

All reviews are greatly appreciated.

Follow me on Facebook or BookBub

https://www.facebook.com/snorthousebooks/

https://partners.bookbub.com/authors/5007629

Visit my website: www.snorthouse.com

THE SHOOTING STAR SERIES

LOVE IS THE GOAL - EXCERPT

I'm standing in the reception area of the Yorkshire Evening Standard as I try to capture the receptionist's attention. The building is made of pebble-dashed concrete and walls of glass. It looked quite modern when it was first built in the early seventies, but now, it is a bit of a carbuncle. The place is humming and I like it. It emits an energy and excitement that makes me feel alive. It's like a train station or an airport. People coming and going, parcels being delivered while others are picked up and loaded into the back of waiting vans. Phones ring non-stop. There's constant chatter.

'Can I help you?' the receptionist asks.

'Yes, I'm here to see Mr Carmichael to collect my press pass.' She looks down her nose at me, as though how could I possibly have any business with the great Bulldog himself.

'Name?' she barks.

'Jimmy, Jimmy Hooper.' She picks up the phone and lets it ring for about two seconds, then says,

'Sorry, he's busy. Can I try someone else?'

'Yes, try Dave Dee.' I get the same response and she is losing patience. 'Okay, try Marky, sorry, Mark Carlyle.'

'Mark, there's a gentleman here to see you by the name … yes, that's right, Jimmy. Okay, I'll send him right up.' She points at some stairs behind her. 'Second floor, turn left at the top, head through the double doors straight ahead.' I scamper up two flights of stairs and burst through into a cavernous open-plan office. Marky comes up to me beaming and holds out his clenched fist.

'Comrade, winning the battle?' I tap my fist into his and pat him on the shoulder.

'Baby steps, Marky, baby steps.'

Marky spends the next twenty minutes walking me around the room introducing me to everyone, many of whom I'd already met the night before. They all shake my hand warmly and make me feel welcome as Marky not only sings my praises but makes me out to be the next David Hockney. Everyone seems to love Marky, and why wouldn't they? He is a life-force, an unbridled fireball of nervous energy that seems to rub off on everyone he talks to.

He then takes me up a floor and we meet and greet all the girls and women from the classified ads department. Same result; all welcoming, all enamoured with Marky. Finally, he takes me down three flights of stairs, at breakneck speed and into the print room. There is a busy hum in the distance as print rollers spin around and print off thousands of copies of tonight's edition of the Standard. There are more introductions before Marky finally finds his man.

'Hey, Jack. This is Jimmy, I was telling you about.' He then puts his hand over his mouth and whispers. 'He's the new photographer. How'd you go with the business cards?' I shake Jack's hand and he looks around surreptitiously.

'Nice to meet you, Jim. Come on boys, follow me.' He leads us past a whole gaggle of typesetters busy at work then into a back room and closes the door. He opens a desk drawer and pulls out four cardboard packages wrapped in brown paper. 'Here you go, Jim.' He hands me the parcels and I slip my backpack off and drop them inside. Marky pulls out a fiver from a bunch of notes and hands it to Jack who quickly tucks it into his back pocket.

'Cheers, Jack. You're a star. Next time I see you in the Soldiers, I'll shout you a few pints,' says Marky.

'Aye, no worries, Marky. Just watch out for security. They've been having a bit of a crackdown, lately. Apparently, a lot of pilfering has been going on. Some people would rob their own grandmother.' Marky laughs as he pats Jack on the shoulder.

'Right, come on Jimmy, back to the control centre.'

##

'Okay, let's go see Dave Dee and get your press pass,' says Marky, once we are back in the hustle and bustle of the newsroom. We head towards an empty desk that is situated at the far end of the room. On the way, an older guy emerges from a doorway.

'Oh, fuck,' says Marky. 'That's John Arnold, resident photographer and the most boring man on the planet. I'll give you fair warning now, Jimmy, do not get into conversations with him or show the slightest interest in what he's got to say, otherwise he will bore your tits off for a good hour. Plus, once he thinks you're his mate, he'll follow you around like a lost puppy.' John Arnold makes a bee-line for us. 'Here he comes, incoming boredom missile,' whispers Marky.

'Hey, Marky, who's the new kid?' says Arnold in a slow, northern drawl.

'John, let me introduce you to Jimmy. Jimmy, here, is a brilliant photographer and is going to be doing a bit of work for us… you know, all the shit you hate doing. The local bands, the acts who come to town on their way up, the bands that come to town on their way down.' Arnold eyes me suspiciously for a moment as he looks me up and down.

'What camera do you use?' he asks.

'Olympus, om10,' I reply, with a gracious smile. He sniffs.

'My go-to is the "Nikon FA". Brilliant bit of engineering. I used to use the Olympus but found it a bit too… granular.'

'That's what I love about it,' I reply. 'It's what give images their humanity. After all, no-one is perfect. I like to capture life, as it is—warts and all.'

'Jimmy is great at capturing faces and iconic images. He's a real artist,' gushes Marky. Arnold sniffs again as he jerks his head upwards.

'Hmm, well, in this game, what the people want is a clear photo, not some arty interpretation, you'd do well to remember that. Are you full-time, part-time or freelance? No-one's said nowt to me about you starting work here, and I am chief photographer,' he inquires, still looking at me warily. Marky laughs.

'Don't worry John, no-one is taking your spot. Jimmy is just doing a bit of freelance, gratis, for a month, just to see how it goes.' Arnold softens his stance and holds out his hand.

'Well, pleased to meet you, Jimmy. We must get together at some point and discuss cameras.' His handshake is limp and weak. He has appalling dandruff and is dressed like some bad actor from 1973, with flared trousers, a wide-collared shirt and a Laurel and Hardy tank-top. Cutting street edge, he is not—although, these are strange fashion times we live in. Marky spots Dave Dee returning to his desk just as Arnold starts up again.

'Sorry, John, but we really do need to speak with Dave. Catch you later. Oh, by the way, didn't see you in the Soldiers last night?' Arnold looks slightly disappointed, then, with his somnambulistic drawl, he replies,

'No, the old ulcer is playing up again. Doc says I have to keep off the grog indefinitely, otherwise, I could die.'

'You worry too much, John. It's not the drinking that gives you ulcers, it's stress. If you can't stand the heat, get out of the kitchen!' Marky pulls me away and we make our way over to Dave Dee. We stand in front of him like schoolboys in the Headmaster's office. He has his head down and is frantically going over some copy, crossing things out, then adding extras. A half-smoked cigarette lays in an ashtray to the side of him, silently burning away. After about thirty seconds he stops scribbling and pushes his notes aside. He looks up at us.

'Sit, sit!' he commands. We both pull out chairs and take a seat. He pulls open his top drawer, throws a couple of laminated cards across the desk and hands me a small box similar to the ones I just collected from Jack in the print room.

'Okay, Jimmy, here's your press pass, security pass and a box of business cards. First of all, security pass is required for out-of-hours entry to the building. Before 7 am and after 9 pm. The press pass will get you into most places; University, Polytechnic, Duke Of York, Irish Club, etc, etc.' He now produces an A4 sheet. 'Take this. Here are the contact names and numbers of all the entertainment venues in Leeds and surrounding areas. Mid-morning, Monday, ring all the venues and make an appointment to meet the manager or whoever's in charge. Go introduce yourself and give them your business card, that way they know you're legit. It always pays to put a face to a name.' I pick the cards up and study them before slipping them into my back pocket along with the sheet of contacts. I grab the box of business cards and chuck them into my backpack.

'Cheers, Dave,' I say. 'This all been okayed by Bulldog?' Dave looks at me sternly.

'It's Mr Carmichael to you and don't forget it. And yes, Bulldog has signed off on it all.' He then pushes another sheet of paper my way.

'These are the acts that are playing in the next month. Thirty of the buggers to entertain this sad and sorry fucking town. I've highlighted the ones I want reviews for in green. As for the others, well, I'll leave that up to you. I want good original photos and copy, not the usual shit we get from their PR office. Right, I'll give you a fair crack of the whip for one month and see how you go. If I like the cut of your jib, then we'll take it from there. We'll supply you with film and you'll have access to all our facilities, including the darkroom, at any time. See John Arnold on the way out and he'll give you some rolls of film, make sure you sign for them. Oh, and remember, the film and darkroom are for work related to the Standard. Don't try using it for your own work—understand?'

'Sure,' I reply as he takes a deep toke on his cigarette. He stands up. He is solid, well-built, a naturally powerful man. He turns and opens a grey filing cabinet behind him and pulls out a bottle of whiskey and three small tumblers. He unscrews the cap and fills the glasses with a small shot of the amber liquid then hands them out.

'Here's to the future! If you are half as good as Marky makes out, then you'll do all right.' We all clink glasses.

'Thanks, Dave, I appreciate you giving me a go. Chances are hard to come by these days.' He sits back down and is immediately consumed with more important matters. He looks at his watch as I check the clock on the wall behind him. 4:55 pm, I have already been here for two hours.

'Have you got wheels?' he asks, as an afterthought. I shake my head in response. He pulls a bulging wallet out of his back pocket, opens it and hands me a twenty. 'This is for bus fares, should keep you going for a month. Keep the ticket stubs, we can claim it back on expenses. If you run short, come and see me. Okay, now fuck off you two. Oh, wait a minute. Marky, are you up for a bit of overtime tomorrow?' Marky grins.

'A Saturday—double time—of course. What's the go?'

'Got a phone call a few minutes ago. Post Office in Armley, armed robbery—bastards! Go around there tomorrow morning and interview the Post Office Master and his wife. Get some details of how and what occurred. Go gentle… they're both shaken up… in their sixties. Then get yourself over to Milgarth Police Station and ask to speak with DCI Willis for a statement. He'll be expecting you. They're putting together a photofit. A lot of fucking use that will be. Two blokes with balaclavas over their heads. Anyway, I want a good photo of the couple … you know… shaken and afraid.'

'Hey, how about I take Jimmy with me to get the photos? He's brilliant at faces?' Dave stares at him, slightly annoyed.

'No! Take the coffin dodger, he's our official photographer.' Marky turns around and looks at John Arnold who is slicing something up on a guillotine.

'Hey, John!' Marky shouts, 'you up for a bit of double-time tomorrow?' Arnold shakes his head.

'Sorry, no can do. Got a wedding. Can't get out of something like that at short notice.' Marky turns back to Dave and smiles. Dave slumps back in his chair.

'Fuck it! Okay, take Jimmy with you. I'm trusting you both. Take a pool car, Marky, and don't prang it.' Dave rips a piece of paper off a notepad and hands it to Marky. 'Here's the details. I need the copy and a good photo on my desk by noon at the latest.'

'Not a problem, Dave, have I ever let you down yet?' grins Marky. We turn and walk away as Dave calls out again.

'Oh, by the way, Marky, you're doing okay—keep it up and you'll soon have my job!'

'I wouldn't want your job for all the tea in China. What time will you knock off tonight?' Marky laughs. Dave stares at his inbox.

'Oh, probably about ten. Then back here tomorrow at eight. It comes with the territory. Okay, now fuck off and let me get on with my work. Have a good night!' We head back over to John Arnold.

'Right, Jimmy, you get sorted with John and I'll just tidy my desk up then we'll head off for a couple of pints.'

'You after some rolls of film?' John asks in a slightly bored manner.

'Yeah, Dave said to see you.'

'Okay, follow me.' He opens the door he'd emerged from earlier and takes me into a large storage room. At the far end is a solid looking door, with a red light above it and signage that reads, "Do not enter when red light is on".

'I take it that's the darkroom?' I say, nodding towards it.

'I see you're a bit of a livewire,' he replies sarcastically. 'How many rolls do you want?'

'Oh, give me ten. That should keep me going for a while.' He slides a box from a shelf and places it on a desk.

'Here, help yourself.' He then pulls a folder out and places it beside the box of film. 'Make sure you sign for it, otherwise, there'll be hell to pay. Time, date, name, amount of film, type of film and reason. Never used to be like this. Anyone could just walk in here and help themselves to whatever. A perk of the job. This last eighteen months they've been cracking down on everything. You can't wipe your arse without them wanting to know how many sheets you've used.'

'This is all black and white. Do you have any colour?' He stares at me with a puzzled look.

'If you hadn't noticed, the fucking newspaper is black and white.'

'The entertainment guide in Saturday's edition is in colour—if you hadn't noticed,' I reply, cockily.

'Smartarse,' he retorts and pulls another box from the shelf. I grab four rolls, lob them into my backpack along with the black and white film then fill out the register. 'Do you want to have a look inside the darkroom?' he offers, expectantly.

'I'd love to John, but I need to make tracks. How about Monday afternoon?' He smiles.

'Aye, okay then—that's if I'm around. You never know what can crop up working here.'

I meet back up with Marky in the main office and we head down the stairs then into the daylight and the city noise.

##

We're sitting in Tossers sipping on our pints laughing and joking at the turn of events.

'I can't believe it, Marky. Just over twenty-four hours ago I was sitting here with you, unemployed, unemployable and nothing on the horizon but signing on and applying for crappy jobs. Now, I have my own press card, a bag full of film, more business cards than you can shake a stick at and a bit of cash in my pocket. Things are looking up and it's all down to you.' Marky laughs and pats me on the arms.

'No, comrade, it's down to you. I just gave you the kick up the arse you needed. You've now officially joined the club, you're part of the gang.'

'What gang?'

'The Evening Standard gang. Dave Dee—he likes you. Once you've got your foot in the door then you are in for good. It's like a giant family working there and they look after their own.' I take a gulp of beer then place it down on a beer mat.

94

'I think it's a bit early to say that, Marky. I need to prove myself first.'

'And you will, my son, you will. Listen, I've barely eaten a thing all day, why don't we head up to the Taj Mahal for a stinking hot curry then come back here and meet the others later.' Macca, Jonesy and Gerry won't show up for another two hours and I am feeling ravenous. Plus, it will be nice and quiet in the Taj at this time of day and I want to tell Marky about the Ice Queen.

'Okay, sounds like a good idea. Sup up your beer and let's make a move.'

##

We've just finished onion bhaji starters and are waiting on our main courses.

'So, what did you get up to last night after you left the Soldiers?' I ask Marky, as he's busy poking his teeth with a toothpick.

'Can't say, mate. I'd like to tell you but it's all hush-hush at the moment. You'll find out one day.' I laugh.

'Fucking hell, Marky, it's all a bit clandestine, a bit cloak-and-dagger. Is this to do with the "struggle" and the "glorious revolution"? I thought you were just playing it up to get a wind up out of us, but you're serious aren't you?' He puts the toothpick down and leans forward with a frown on his face.

'Oh, yes, I'm serious all right.' He shoots a glance around the restaurant. 'There are forces at play right now. Things are going to change—big time,' he says softly. He worries me. I decide to change the subject.

'You want to know what I got up to last night when I left you?'

'Yeah, of course, I do.'

'I went to the Granary. There was a band playing and I got some shots of them. Met the lead singer's girlfriend and gave her my card. She came round to my place today and collected some prints.' He's nodding as I speak. 'She gave me a blowjob in my darkroom, payment in kind if you will.' Marky grins.

'You dirty little fucker. Don't you feel bad fucking someone else's girl?'

'I didn't fuck her. It was just a blowjob—and yes I did feel a little uneasy but before I knew it she had unzipped me and had me in her mouth. There's no turning back at that point.'

'No, I guess not.' The waiter arrives with our curries and plates of chapattis. We waste no time in tucking in.

'Anyway, that's not the only thing that happened.'

'Go on,' he says, his attention now firmly fixed on his beef madras.

'Well, in the Granary, before I met the girl from the band, I also met another girl in the upstairs bar.'

'Fuck! You can't leave it alone can you,' he mumbles as he stuffs a big piece of chapatti into his mouth.

'The thing is, Marky, I'm in love.'

'Yeah, sure you are.'

'No, I mean it. This girl was… is… the most beautiful girl on the planet. Her looks are breathtaking and I fell for her straight away.' Marky still seems more interested in eating than my tale of love.

'What's her name?'

'Victoria. I tried all my Jimmy Hooper charm on her and she threw it all back in my face. Couldn't even get her to crack a smile. Plus, she's super posh, I mean like royalty posh.' That got his attention. He places his fork down on the table and dabs at the sides of his mouth with a napkin.

'Forget about her, Jimmy. It will never work. You are going to open yourself up to a world of pain. I've told you about their type before. I'm telling you, Jimmy, those bastards will never let you into their private club. No matter what you do, no matter what you strive for, no matter what you achieve, you will always be a commoner to them—less than zero. They believe they were born to rule and you were born to be their mule Walk away from it right now.' I stare at him for a few seconds.

'I can't. There's something about her which electrifies me. This isn't lust or wanting something I can't have—it's different—something I've never felt before. Even talking about her now, I'm getting goosebumps, my hands are tingling and I'm getting the biggest boner on.'

'Oh, for God's sake man! Show some respect, I'm eating here! Jim, listen to me, this will end in tears. She will chew you up and spit you out when she's ready, once she's had her bit of "rough". She'll break your fucking heart, man! And, you know what you're like, you love too much, you feel too much—you're an emotional sponge.'

'Well, I'm willing to take that risk. In fact, I've taken a vow of celibacy. No more sex with anyone until I've made love to her. Now I think about it, she will be the only woman I have sex with for the rest of my life.' Marky leans back in his chair and takes a large gulp of beer.

'This place does one of the best curries in the city but their beer is shit! So, your vow of celibacy didn't last long, did it?' I'm not sure what he means.

'Come again?'

'Quite. Well, you take this vow of celibacy and less than twelve hours later you're getting gobbled off in your darkroom. There goes that vow.' I pause for thought. He's right, I've failed straight away.

'Well, the vow of celibacy starts right here and now.'

'Do you understand what celibacy means?'

'I'm not stupid. It means abstaining from sex.'

'Yep, any sex. And that includes having a wank. Are you telling me that you are never going to knock one out for the rest of your life?' I haven't contemplated this—but now I do—I'm feeling strong.

'Well, not for the rest of my natural. Once I've made love to Victoria, then self-abuse can resume on a normal twice-daily basis.' Marky chuckles then looks thoughtfully at me.

'If she gave you the brush off last night, what makes you think next time will be any different?'

'Not sure. Yes, she did give me the cold shoulder but there was something else, I can't explain it. I got this feeling like we'd been together once before in a previous life. There was this overwhelming feeling of sadness, of melancholy, yet wrapped in deep love.' Marky laughs.

'Fuck me drunk! You've been reading too many of those romantic poets. Well, James, my boy, it's your call. But don't say I didn't warn you. And remember, I'm your best mate, so when your heart is laying in tattered pieces on the floor, I'll be here to help you stitch it back together.'

'Hey, don't mention this to the others—right?'

'Okay, if you say so.'

END OF "LOVE IS THE GOAL" EXCERPT

BUY NOW

ABOUT THE AUTHOR

Simon Northouse writes books that entertain. His stories include hefty doses of self-deprecating satire, ironic farce and droll bathos delivered in a deadpan Yorkshire voice. However, as many of his fans have pointed out, there is much, *much* more to his books than laughter.

He touches on social issues that have plagued humans since the first man pointed at a woman on the back of a woolly mammoth and shouted, "Oi, love, come down from there. That's a man's job!" Racism, misogyny, sexism, elitism, classism, anxiety, self-doubt and entitlement are just a sprinkling of issues that intersperse his works.

He's also big on love, mateship, truth and loyalty and their darker flip sides. Yes, there is humour, bonding, ridiculous situations and tender touching moments of true feeling that live alongside each other on the page. His philosophy is simple, *entertain!*

Oh, and lastly, Simon Northouse is not a New York Times or USA Today bestselling author. He has yet to be nominated for the Booker Prize or Miles Franklin Award and he is still waiting on a call from the Nobel Foundation—the clock is ticking, people.

He is the author of the Soul Love, The Shooting Star and School Days series. He also puts out a cracking monthly newsletter which you can find by just typing, "Discombobulated Newsletter" into your web search engine—I kid you not!